HONEST REDEMPTION

Phillip Davis

HOG PRESS

Hog Press
an imprint of Culicidae Press®
PO Box 5069
Madison, WI 53705-5069
hogpress.com
editor@hogpress.com

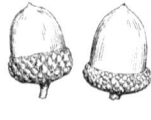

HOG PRESS

ISBN: 978-1-68315-145-6

Our books may be purchased in bulk for promotional, educational
or business use. Please contact your local bookseller or the
Culicidae Press Sales Department at +1-352-215-7558
or by email at sales@culicidaepress.com

culicidaepress.bsky.social – facebook.com/culicidaepress
threads.net/@culicidaepress – instagram.com/culicidaepress
x.com/culicidaepress

Design by polytekton © 2025
Cover image generated by Midjourney AI system and modified by
polytekton

Table of Contents

CHAPTER 1
Meet Jason Jennings

Leaving Windsor, Ontario. Jason Jennings was heading through the Detroit-Windsor Tunnel and in two and a half miles he would be back in the United States. Jason was a very dedicated over-the-road truck driver who has been in the employment of Staley Trucking and Warehousing, LLC for over fifteen years now. He is the company owner, Brice Staley's, top performer, and most dedicated employee. Jason would handle loads other drivers would not or preferred not to handle. He was the sole breadwinner for his home as his wife, Lindsey, was busy taking care of their home and two young children in Atlanta, Georgia. Their daughters, April and Lauren, ages seven and four, were the pieces of the puzzle which completed Jason's life. He hated the hours away from them while he was on the road, but he had a passion for trucking and his wife, and young daughters supported him unconditionally.

Jason was exhausted from this most recent trip and was still eleven hours away from Memphis, Tennessee where he was to deliver this container of cargo. The Staleys owned a substantial number of warehouses and over the road trucks. Memphis was the Staleys largest and most utilized facility as it had a proximity to the FedEx home office and main hub of distribution. The Staley Corporation would repackage and ship some of their products via FedEx to save on transportation fees. Atlanta was another six hours from Memphis so Jason would need to stop along the route soon and rest for the night.

As he pulled into a travel stop and fuel center to have a quick bite to eat and return to his rig, which was equipped with a rear sleeper, he laughed an exhausted laugh to himself about the day's events at the warehouse in Windsor, Ontario. He arrived early for his appointment, which was customary for him. Jason prided himself on his promptness, dedication, and organization. The dockworkers at the warehouse began to load him on time, which was not necessarily customary in his industry and Jason was pleasantly surprised. As they were wrapping up the loading of the crated material, the team suddenly began to remove labeling from certain crates, remove those crates, and reattach the labeling to another set of crates. Jason had his manifest and would verify the crates and ensure the proper international labeling was attached but the contents of the crates were to be verified by this warehousing facility and their personnel. Jason's job was to ensure the material was roadworthy and the number of skids and crates were accurate. The process continued to be executed, by every estimation, by workers who had no idea what they were to load and even what a warehousing operation was all about. Jason, a patient and understanding man, had become frustrated and asked the warehouse manager to investigate the calamity. The manager, a high-strung and anxious individual asked Jason to come into his office and have a cup of coffee and bagel. Jason attempted to calm the manager, but he began to look out of the office window at the loading team more than he focused on Jason. He finally left Jason sitting in his office and rushed out the door to the loading dock after closing the blinds of the window he was so ardently staring out of. Jason removed his cell phone and began to surf the internet while he awaited this obviously distracted leadership to return. The manager reentered his office forty-five minutes later and appeared more anxious than he did before he left. He explained this was a newly hired crew and apologized repeatedly for the delay and the warehouse's lack of direction. The final loading mercifully ended some eight hours after Jason had arrived, and Jason just thought to himself about how quickly he could get the hell out of there. He hoped he did not have to visit the Windsor facility for an awfully long time to come. His cargo matched his manifest, and the count was correct he thought to himself, and this had to be a victory for that crew. He chuckled again as he drifted off to sleep.

Jason awoke early the next morning and decided to call Brice once he arrived at the Memphis warehouse to unload. He arrived at the Memphis warehouse in about thirty minutes, showed his credentials to the security guard managing the gate, and slowly pulled within the secured warehouse unloading zone. The security guard, Riley Troupe, walked up to Jason as he stepped down from the cab of the rig. Riley extended his hand and Jason shook hands with Riley as he always did upon arrival at the Memphis facility. Riley was a very likable person and never at a loss for words. Jason was hopeful he was not longwinded this morning because he really wanted to get him to Atlanta and see his family.

"Good morning, Jason. How was the trip? It sure has been busy around here for the last couple weeks. I guess everyone is gearing up for their Christmas products and winter sales. I have seen more trucks here the last two weeks than traffic on Interstate 55," Riley spoke as he softly spit tobacco juice on the asphalt beneath his feet.

Jason smiled and gave a hearty chuckle at Riley's weak attempt at humor, "I bet it has been a madhouse around here for you Riley. How many people are in front of me this morning to be offloaded. I spent over eight hours at the Windsor warehouse as those dock workers could not find their asses with both hands. It was mass chaos. The manager stood around and he didn't know whether to scratch his watch or wind his ass. What a day. I am glad to be back in the USA and near home."

"You say you had trouble there, too?" Riley asked as he spit more tobacco juice near his tattered work boots.

"I sure as hell did, my friend. What a joke. I have seen some poorly run operations, but that outfit takes the cake, Jason said as he put both hands on the small of his back and stretched backwards to loosen up his muscles from the night's sleep in the rear of the rig.

Jason began to walk to the rear of the trailer to remove the seal and prepare to back into a dock door for unloading. He looked back at Riley still standing there in his dingy gray coveralls and with his bright red baseball cap pulled slightly sideways with the name of his security company, All-Star Security, in gold lettering across the front. He smiled at Riley and Riley began to walk back towards the guard shack. Jason proceeded to the rear of the trailer and stopped just a few feet from the end of the trailer.

"Riley. Hold up one second please. What did you mean when you asked if I had trouble there, too? If there is a persistent problem there in Windsor, I want to mention it to Brice when I get home to Atlanta. I don't want to cause undo trouble for anyone, but we truckers are not making money unless our wheels are turning. We can't afford to wait eight to ten hours every time we stop there," Jason spoke as he took a couple steps back towards Riley and leaned against the container and chassis connected to his rig.

"Yes sir. I spoke to four or five drivers this week and they all said it was at least a six hour wait as the dockworkers goofed up the crates and labeling. One driver said he asked if he could help and hopped up on the dock to assist and a manager came running out of the office and asked him to step down and return to his rig or the trucker's lounge and wait. This driver said the manager was nervous as a whore in church and looked like a gentle breeze could have blown him over until he stepped off the dock and back into his rig. He sat and watched as they popped open crates, looked inside, sealed the crate, and changed labeling. He was as confused as you were with all the disorganization. He called them all a bunch of dumbasses and hoped he never had to go back there," Riley smiled through his tobacco-stained teeth and tugged at his ball cap.

"Thanks Riley. I will speak with Brice when I get home, and he can investigate. Sounds like they need some housecleaning up there. Can you squeeze me next, please? I want to get home and see my wife and daughters," Jason said as he popped the seal on the container and headed back to the cab of his rig.

"I got you next Jason. Let me know what Mr. Staley has to say. I like you folks and want you all to make plenty of money. It keeps me with a job here."

Riley was a man of his word. He had Jason positioned in the next spot and asked the dockworkers to handle Jason's unload next. The unloading took about an hour. Jason napped off and on until one of the dockworkers tapped on his cab window and gave him a thumbs up. This was a signal the unloading was complete, and Jason could verify his container was empty and head home to Atlanta. Jason pulled up fifteen feet, hopped out and almost ran to the back of the container to verify and be on his way home. He stopped at the guard shack, waved, and mouthed "see you next time" to Riley and slowly pulled out the gate. He hopped on Interstate 55 would take him near Georgia. He would be glad to see Interstate 75 as that would take him home to Atlanta. As he drove along, he thought how he would approach Brice with the Windsor warehouse news and how he hoped Brice could address the problems.

Jason decided to report to the office as he made great time on the drive home and it was now 1:00 PM. He would stop by the Staley central office building, speak with Brice, and ask the dispatcher for his next load. He pulled the rig to a stop alongside the administration building where Brice spent most of his time and climbed out of his rig. Jason was a tall man standing nearly six feet six inches tall and had a medium build. He was not thin but not overweight because his doctor and wife, Lindsey, kept him on a very balanced diet. He rolled up the sleeves of his plaid flannel shirt, ran his fingers through his jet-black hair, and pushed a wrinkle or two out of his blue jeans as he walked toward the main entrance of the administration building. He walked in and greeted the very pretty, blonde receptionist, Kelly Parton. He asked if Brice was in and if he was busy. Kelly smiled politely, shook her head no about Brice being busy, and pointed to Brice's office door down the hall. Jason waved at Kelly, tapped her mahogany name holder on her desk as he walked by which read on the gold name plate 'the queen', in small lettering underneath her name. This was a special gift from Brice years ago to Kelly. Jason continued his stroll down the hallway toward Brice's office. Kelly was recognized as the best point of contact at the office because she practically held the operation together. Brice would pay almost any salary request she had as she was just that pivotal to the success of the operation. Jason rapped on Brice's office door and a voice on the other side asked him to come in.

"I see you making another million-dollar decision today, Mr. Staley. I admire how you wheel and deal and make it all happen. I am sorry to stop in during the middle of the day, but I had something I wanted to speak with you about. If you have a few minutes," Jason beamed brightly as he walked over to Brice's desk and shook his hand.

"I always have time for the man who is not only my best driver, but also the fullest of shit guy on my payroll. If I didn't have to pay your fat ass salary, I could maybe retire someday. Please have a seat and let's talk," Brice pushed away from his desk slightly, folded his hands, and gave Jason his undivided attention.

"I am not much of a complainer, Brice, but something happened up in Windsor a couple days ago and I found out it was not just an issue for me but a few other of your drivers," Jason said almost apologetically as he had a seat in the leather back chair across from Brice's desk.

Jason took a deep breath and slowly exhaled. "Brice, I had some issues at the Windsor warehouse location I just picked up from a couple of days ago. As a trucker, we have all experienced issues getting loaded and our freight not always matching the manifest. This warehouse was the worst and the leadership there was so high-strung I am not sure he has still come back down to Earth. The dock crew made multiple changes of crates and labeling and loaded and unloaded several times. I don't mind being patient and human error happening, but this was the most unorganized scene I have ever witnessed. I am not upset about the time wasted as I am a company guy and want to make you and I both profitable. What does concern me is that when I spoke with Riley at the Memphis location, he said something that made me think. Riley asked me if I had trouble there, too. We spoke about it and there seems to be a trend of excess movement and inept ability there, Brice. I am not asking that we terminate business with them or even launch a documented complaint but I know you do a lot of business with and have a solid reputation with the owners there and just thought you may like to ask a few questions." Jason moved forward slightly in his chair as he spoke and lowered his head as if he were apologizing to Brice.

"Jason, you are one of the best, if not the top driver we have in this organization. I tease you a lot because we have that type of relationship. Please do not feel bad for bringing this to my attention or trying to better this business. I am thankful for the information, and I do have a relationship with the ownership there in Windsor. You have my word that I will speak with them in strictest confidence to see if they can drill down on what the oddities might be and how they can correct their operation. If it were a one-off instance, it could be dismissed but this sounds more like the norm of their operation and not a set of isolated instances from one stop. Give me a few days and I promise I will give you an update," Brice spoke sincerely as he nodded affirmation towards Jason.

Glancing down at a schedule he had on his desk, Brice looked back up at Jason. "It looks like you are heading over to Houston the day after tomorrow to drop off a container at the port there and will grab another container heading to Windsor. I will have an update for you before you leave Houston. If you have similar issues at the Windsor facility again, call me right away. I know you are not one to seek out trouble, but I want to address any other issue in real time. Now get your ass out of here and get home to those three pretty ladies of yours. You deserve the rest, and I am tired of looking at you," Brice cracked a huge smile and laughed as he spoke.

Jason stood up laughed a big laugh and shook Brice's hand. He whispered "Thank you" as he turned toward the door and headed for his rig. He climbed inside, fired the engine, and shifted into drive. He was heading home and was ready to spend a couple of days with his family.

Lindsey met him at the door as she had seen Jason pull up alongside their home in the vacant lot beside their property. The Jennings had planned with the owner of the vacant lot to use it for parking and offered to pay but the owner of the lot would not hear of it because he knew Jason would be respectful of the property and it would be nice to have some visibility there as the owner did not want to have hobos take up residence there. Jason almost ran up the driveway to embrace his wife and he scooped her up and kissed her as if he hadn't seen her in weeks when it had only been a few days. As they were saying their hellos, love you, and welcome home, out raced two young ladies in matching outfits but not quite fitting well. April and Lauren enjoyed playing dress up and doing the activity themselves, but they had gotten their wardrobes mixed this particular morning. April, the oldest and taller of the two, had grabbed her sister Lauren's top and her own jeans. April was jumping up and down at her daddy's feet as was her sister. April's shirt was about chest length and Lauren's was almost knee length. They couldn't care less, and Jason felt the same way. He scooped up his daughters, one in each arm, and kissed each of them as he followed his wife inside their home. The girls smiled and kissed their daddy as he collapsed on the sofa, still gripping his daughters close to his chest.

"You need to get a hot shower and come downstairs, fall in your recliner, and relax while the girls and I make you a hot, homemade meal," Lindsey insisted as she smiled at Jason. The girls always missed Jason and were so excited each time he arrived home after having been on an extended run.

"No argument from me on that one," Jason said as he made his way to the stairs to their bedroom and shower area. "One request, however. I get to choose my clothing and dress myself. You dropped the ball on the girls today.

Lindsey tossed a dish towel at Jason as he sprinted up the stairs and he and Lindsey both laughed at the obvious.

CHAPTER 2

The Return to Windsor, Ontario

The night and day off passed quickly for Jason and the time had raced more quickly as his wife Lindsey and his daughters were concerned. As the ladies in his life traditionally did, they walked Jason to his rig while he carried one of his daughters and held his wife's hand as the other daughter clung to the leg of his blue jeans as she tried to keep pace walking down the driveway. Jason kissed his wife and hugged her for several seconds. Jason loved his job and the secure finances it provided for his family but some days he wished he had a weekly 9:00 AM to 5:00 PM career so he could be at home each night. He missed the nights sleeping alongside his wife and waking up to his daughters bouncing on his bed anxious for him to get up and spend time with them. He also missed his best friend, Ronald Watts. Ronald was the sheriff of Glynn County in Georgia and was one of the most sought-after law enforcement officers in the state. Ronald had made a name for himself in a high-profile case several years ago involving the location of a missing Glynn County District Attorney. Sheriff Watts had no desire to leave his native Glynn County as he loved the Brunswick area and more importantly the beautiful Golden Isles which neighbored Brunswick. Little did Jason or Ronald know that their paths would soon cross and not necessarily for the best.

Jason arrived at Staley's Trucking and slowly backed under the chassis of his load going to the port of Houston. As promised, Brice met him in the yard as Jason was performing his pre-trip inspection of the chassis, container, and his bill of lading. Jason meticulously checked every point on the safety checklist which was required by the DOT and enforced by Staley Trucking. Jason would handle the official electronic input of the checklist on the unit inside the cab of his rig, but he always kept a paper backup for his records in case he was stopped by the DOT, or a check was performed at a weigh station.

"What the hell is going on with Jason," Brice said as Jason walked towards him with his hand extended to shake his friend's hand.

"Good morning, buddy. I am trying to get rolling. I must make a meager living for my family and me while I get my boss rich with every container load. This pot of gold for Staley Trucking is heading to Houston and then I take a container from the port there full of gold to Windsor. My boss at Saley getting richer by the second," Jason smiled as he could not resist the opportunity to tease Brice.

"How about kissing my rosy ass, Jason," Brice smiled and winked at Jason. "I wanted to personally come out and see you and discuss the situation at Windsor. I spoke with the leadership at the facility there and explained we were concerned about the operations and wanted to attempt to understand the bottlenecks occurring there. A gentlemen named Rowland Davis, who is the operations manager in Windsor, assured me he has fielded more than one complaint about the lackluster performance of the team there and has met with them, He has stressed to the team that a continuation of the current performance would lead to changes in middle-level leadership at the facility as well as significant turnover in general labor, as needed. Rowland was genuinely concerned about your observations and other drivers who have loaded and unloaded in Windsor. He has agreed to meet you at the dock upon your arrival and personally observe the loading and dispatch of your outgoing container. We spoke for almost an hour yesterday and I could tell by the tone of his voice that he was not a happy camper with his team. I can almost assure you things will be handled much more smoothly there moving forward. His assistant operations manager told me they called him "colonel" at the facility and did not enjoy his oversight on day-to-day operations. I think he handles things a little more sternly than they enjoy. I explained to him you were just an overpaid, spoiled ass, crybaby, but he insisted on helping you out," Brice took one last jab at Jason before he let him ride out.

"Now it is my turn to say, 'kiss my ass.' I genuinely appreciate you calling him. I am not trying to be problematic. It was just a junior league joke of an operation when I was there the last time. I have seen some bush-league leadership, this leadership included, but my gosh," Jason tapped Brice on the shoulder as he smiled and walked toward the cab of his rig. He could not resist trying to get the last word in the continuous joshing the two men enjoyed.

Jason climbed up the steps of his rig and opened the driver's door. He looked back and smiled and waved at his friend and employer. Brice gave Jason the finger and smiled as he mouthed "be safe asshole" as Jason disappeared into the cab of his rig. Jason fired the engine, raised the fifth wheel on the chassis, released the brakes, and slowly began to pull through the gate of Staley Trucking en route to the Port of Houston.

Jason arrived at the Port of Houston and dropped the container he had hauled from Georgia and was directed by the port's assistant manager of container operations to yard perpendicular to where he had just delivered his container. Jason proceeded to the yard and began to search for the trailer number listed on his manifest. He spotted the container and began backing underneath the chassis. As he was almost connected to the chassis and fifth wheel, a port employee came running feverishly up to his rig and waving a printed manifest. She motioned for Jason to stop and moved her hands in such a way as to ask him to roll down his driver's side window. Jason stopped as instructed and hit the button to roll down his window as he simultaneously shifted his rig into park. He stuck his head out of the window and directed his attention to the young lady standing below his door.

"Sir, my name is Melanie Leaky, and I am the assistant manager of container operations for this yard. We made a mistake issuing this container and we need you to deliver another trailer to the Windsor location."

Jason, looking puzzled at Melanie, spoke inquisitively. "Ma'am, this manifest was generated by my dispatcher back in Georgia and I have not received a call from anyone at my office requesting I change container numbers. The dispatcher or my boss, Brice Staley, would have alerted me to the change. Are you sure I am the person who needs to pick up this newly issued container?"

"Yes sir. We spoke with Mr. Staley, and he is aware of the change and has agreed to allow you to transport the new container to Windsor. If you would like to call him, please do."

"Give me one second please and I would like to call him." Jason was gathering his cell phone from the passenger seat and began to dial Brice's cell number. Brice answered on the second ring and Jason began to ask him about the change and why no one contacted him sooner. Jason explained that he was almost hooked to the container on the manifest he was given in Georgia and may have left with it and not this new container. Brice apologized and asked Jason to accept the new container and its final destination was Windsor so he would not need to change routes just containers as this freight was needed more urgently than the previously assigned container. Jason was cooperative as always and told Brice he would handle it and see him in a few days back in Georgia.

"Mr. Staley did say I needed to take the new container as the freight was needed more urgently. Where is this container located and I will take care of it." Melanie pointed out the container which was located on the opposite aisle but in the same yard. She explained that she would meet Jason over at the container and ensure the chassis and container were in sound condition.

As Melanie began to walk back to her yard transportation vehicle, Jason began driving his rig over to the new container and backed underneath the chassis and connected the fifth wheel. He climbed down from his rig and made his way toward the rear of the container as he was going to open the container and verify that it was indeed loaded and verify the contents based on the manifest he was about to receive from Melanie. He remembered his bolt cutters were in the toolbox underneath his driver's side door and turned back to grab them as he knew the container would be locked. He would get another lock from Melanie or the guard gate before he hit the interstate. As he made his way to the rear of the container, he could hear Melanie's transport vehicle race louder as she screeched alongside his rig in a flash and jumped out of the vehicle before it had come to a complete stop.

'What are you going to do with those bolt cutters," Melanie shrieked as she literally ran up to where Jason was standing.

"I am going to cut the lock and verify the contents and you or your security team can issue me another lock afterwards," Jason was trying not to be sarcastic as this was standard procedure and felt Melanie should be familiar with the process.

"I am sorry. That was a silly question. I am just overwhelmed today and being pulled in one hundred different directions. We unfortunately cannot cut the lock on the load. It has a C-TPAT (Customs-Trade Partnership Against Terrorism) lock, and I am a little embarrassed to admit that our admins neglected to order replacement locks, and they are not due in until this afternoon."

Jason stood frozen in his tracks and looked bewildered at Melanie. "I am not very comfortable not being able to verify the contents against the manifest. Isn't there something we can do? I know C-TPAT locks must be replaced with the same type locks, and they differ from standard locks for normal loads, but I am very uneasy about this."

"As you know sir, we are certified under C-TPAT regulations and are authorized to verify contents and lock the containers down. I assure you the freight has been verified and is correct. We cannot cut this lock. Quinn from your organization has taken C-TPAT loads from us under similar conditions. Actually, he is the person who handles most, if not all, of the C-TPAT containers traveling to Windsor," Melanie had begun to speak with a voice of defiance.

"Ok. I did not mean to upset you and I am not questioning anyone's authority or integrity. It is just the way I have always liked to handle containers, but I will check the chassis and trailer for damage and be on my way. I know Quinn and he is a great guy and solid driver. I am sure you all love working with him," Jason sighed and spoke with an apologetic tone.

"I am so sorry, AGAIN. I did not mean to snap at you. I have had a rotten day and now I am trying to vent my frustration on someone who just likes to be efficient. Please accept my apologies."

Jason smiled at Melanie as he assured her no apologies were needed and he appreciated her assistance. He made a thorough check of the chassis and exterior of the container and uncovered no issues. He climbed into the rig and waved goodbye to Melanie and made his way toward the guard checkpoint to pass along the signed copy of the manifest for their records. The security team processed his exit quickly and he was on his way up north to Windsor. As he drove along, he was still in amazement how a facility the size of the Port of Houston could run out of C-TPAT locks. What a Mickey Mouse operation he thought to himself. He was grateful this was Quinn Brown's normal route and not his.

The miles clicked away as did the hours. Jason was beginning to tire and decided to stop at the next rest area he came to. He made great time on the interstate today and he would get a good night's rest. He was now in Michigan and would not have to travel far tomorrow to be in Windsor. He saw a sign up ahead that said the next rest stop is three miles away. He took the exit and located a well-lit place to park his rig and load and parked for the evening. Jason climbed in the sleeper section of his rig, called his wife to say he loved them and good night, and he drifted off to sleep.

He awoke the next morning just as the sun had begun to peak over the oak trees which lined the rest stop. The tunnel traffic was moving smoothly, and Jason was making excellent time. He was listening to his radio which was tuned in on the classic 1980's station. His wife made fun of him telling him he was trying to recapture his youth and he also was a terrible singer. Jason did not care and if a good AC/DC tune came on he would crank up the volume and sing all the words along with the band. He was also thinking about the impending visit to the Windsor facility and was saying a silent prayer between chords hoping that all processes went smoothly this morning.

Jason pulled up to the Windsor location's guard shack and stopped short of the electronic gate so he could provide his manifest and credentials to the guard inside the building. The guard scanned the manifest up to the receiving team for processing and informed Jason he was to report to door 201 for immediate verification by the receiving team and the manager of operations would be waiting for him there, as well. The large metal gate slowly opened as it dragged the ground slightly and puffed up a small cloud of dust from the gravel/dirt parking lot. Jason moved slowly through the gate and took a slight turn to the right and saw his assigned door. As he drew closer to the unloading dock, he noticed a distinguished gentleman standing on the dock in a pair of slacks, a pressed long-sleeved dress shirt, and a light blue tie which was tied in a Balthus Knot. The gentleman, obviously the manager of operations, was flanked by a team of warehouse associates on his left and right. Jason circled around and began to back up to his assigned door. His door was just two doors down from the dock where the manager was standing. Jason sighed a little sigh of relief knowing he had someone he believed to be qualified to make this visit and unload and load a smooth one. He slowly inched the door against the dock pad, lowered the fifth, disconnected from the chassis, and slowly pulled forward away from the now disconnected chassis and load. As he slowly exited the cab of his rig, the manager descended the dock steps and made his way towards Jason. The associates who had been flanking him quickly sprang into action and began to unload the freight.

"Good morning, sir, my name is Rowland Davis. I understand there was a series of embarrassing events you encountered with our team on your last visit, and I am here to personally apologize, and I will be on standby to ensure everything, and I mean everything goes smoothly this visit. I am ashamed of our team and their effort and want to assure you this will be a much more favorable experience," Mr. Davis was very professional and adamant in his tone.

"No need to apologize Mr. Davis. These things happen and I just want everyone to learn from these experiences and all of us to become better at our jobs. Our customers depend on all of us, and we depend on them for our salaries. I appreciate your being here and I know things will flow more smoothly today. Please consider it a one-time instance and growth opportunity."

The two men stood and chatted a few more minutes and Jason asked him where the empty container was located so he could bring it back to Staley's for loading. Mr. Davis looked at Jason for a brief second and then stared at the clipboard of paperwork he had been carrying. He flipped through several manifests on the clipboard and then looked back up at Jason.

"An empty," Mr. Davis asked inquisitively?

"Yes sir. The directions I received from my dispatcher at Staley's was to deliver the container I picked up at the Port of Houston, deliver it to Windsor, and then collect an empty container to deliver to Staley's for loading," Jason spoke confidently as he always knew what he was to deliver and collect in advance and doublechecked with his dispatcher before departure.

"Your dispatcher must not have been updated, unfortunately. I spoke with Brice, Mr. Staley, personally yesterday afternoon and he approved the change of containers which you were to haul back to Atlanta."

"I need to speak with Brice. Excuse me for a minute, please," Jason walked away briskly obviously frustrated with another botched set of orders between Staley's and the Windsor site.

Jason stepped away from Rowland about twenty feet to be outside of earshot and dialed Brice's cell phone. He kicked away at the loose gravel in the loading area as the phone began to ring. Brice picked up on the third ring and Jason began to pepper him with questions about the change in containers, the lack of organization here in Windsor, and why he was not notified by at least the dispatcher about the change in containers, if not by Brice himself, if he made the decision to change the loading plan.

"You are the boss, Brice, and I will move whatever you ask me to but I would like some notification as it is obvious these people have no damn clue as what they hope to achieve nor how in the hell they hope to achieve it," Jason was past frustrated and it was spilling over ardently into his conversation with Brice.

"Listen, Jason. I am sorry this has turned into another cluster adventure with this circus. I assumed Mr. Davis would provide some solid leadership, but it appears he is nothing more than the head clown of this three-ring operation. If you would please just grab the container they have assigned to you. They called me yesterday and I want to be honest, I knew it would ruin your night, if I called and told you about the change but I should have called this morning, and I was tied up all morning with calls and meetings. I will make it up to you. I also know how meticulous you are and let me explain the fact that the container is locked, and they are low or out of C-TPAT locks. That place is in a shambles and needs a major overhaul. Please get your container and get the hell out of there. Maybe we can get someone with some stroke there that can correct the dumb shit that is happening there," Brice was visibly upset and apologetic towards his friend and best fleet driver.

"Brice, I am sorry for getting heated but, man, what a crew this operation has. I am also extremely uncomfortable not being able to verify my manifest versus the loading. What I really need is to get on the road and get home to my family. These days here have just been some unbelievable occurrences and mishaps. I am going to travel back into the states and get an early night's rest tonight and head back to Georgia. I will stop in and see you when I get back to Atlanta. Enjoy the rest of your day and I appreciate your letting me vent."

"No apologies needed. I am sincerely not through investigating the calamity and poor leadership and day-to-day operations there in Windsor. I will call you in the morning and check in with you and hopefully a better day is on the horizon for us both."

Jason hung up on the call with Brice and slipped his cell phone back into the shirt pocket of his plaid flannel shirt and made his way back to his rig. He walked back over to Mr. Davis and shook his hand and told him Brice had filled him in on all the container change and he appreciated his time and patience. Mr. Davis assured him it was not an issue and apologized for any confusion. Jason quickly climbed into his rig and fired the engine. He gently pulled the truck into drive and carefully drove toward the guard shack. The guard took a copy of the manifest for their records and opened the departure gate for Jason. Jason managed a small wave of relief as he was finally getting the hell out of this world of confusion and unprofessionalism. He looked back into his driver's side mirror and smiled as the Windsor Warehouse facility was now in the distance.

Jason stopped at a rest station in Ohio later that evening and decided to take his mandatory eight-hour rest and resume the ride to Atlanta in the morning. He ate a cold can of soup, called his wife and daughters, and then climbed into the sleeper section of his rig to get a good night's sleep. He awoke at 4:00 AM and stepped over to the truck stop across the street to have a hot breakfast and grab a shower. He surfed the internet on his cell phone while he enjoyed his bacon, eggs, and coffee. He grabbed a quick, hot shower and made his way back to his rig around 5:15 AM. He checked his truck, chassis, and container to verify everything was in order and the lock was intact on the container. Everything checked out well and he made his way to the driver's side and climbed inside the cab of his rig. He reached out to turn the key and fire up the engine when a text alert popped in on his cell phone. He smiled broadly because he knew it had to be from Lindsey and he was excited she was up a little early today to wish him a great day. He entered the passcode on his cell and opened his text app. Jason's smile slowly changed to a wrinkled forehead as the text was from Brice. Jason opened the text which was asking him to call before he started his drive for the day. Jason thought for a second that it was awfully early for Brice to be up and conducting business, but he called Brice and Brice picked up on the second ring.

"What the hell do I owe the pleasure, boss?"

"Good morning, Jason. I wanted to make sure your lazy ass was up and moving and not billing me for miles and work you are not doing. It seems chasing you has become a fulltime job for me, so I don't have to file for bankruptcy for the all the cash you are milking out of me."

"If I don't get a raise soon, I am going to have to get a part-time job to feed my family. You are getting fat on my labor, and I am not seeing any of the damn profits," Jason had to return the joke back over the fence to Brice.

"Ok, enough of the lies. Let me get to the crux on the matter and let you get rolling. I wanted to start out by saying, please do not shoot the messenger and I am going to reimburse you over and above your normal rate for handling this. Those idiots from Windsor called me last night, in the middle of the damn night, and screwed up again Jason. I am sincerely thinking of suspending business with those guys after this load. I hate to lose business, but this operation is becoming more of a headache than we at Staley's need to deal with. If you need to go home first, I understand, but if you possibly can, I need the container you have to the Port of Laredo. I am so sorry, Jason. You name your price and if you cannot do it, I completely understand. You can bring it to Atlanta, and I will have someone take it from Staley's to Laredo," Brice was obviously disgusted with Windsor at this point and had fire in his voice.

"I'm good, Brice. There is no need to pay me anything extra. You have been good to me, and my family and I am here for both of us to be successful. I am in Ohio now, and I will redirect to Laredo. Please don't give up business in Windsor. I think I may have overblown things and made more of an issue of this than really meets the eye. I will get rolling in a few minutes, if you can email me the new manifest so I can print it out when I get to the port office in Laredo," Jason was the consummate professional and do anything for Brice and Staley Trucking.

"Thanks Jason and the answer is no. I am going to pay you extra wages for this move. You can get Lindsey something special or even get your awesome boss a gift as Boss's Day is rapidly approaching. I am going to look at the Windsor operation and decide on our partnership with them going forward. I truly appreciate you! Have a safe journey and I will email the updated manifest over shortly," Brice was very apologetic in his tone.

"You know what I think I will do with the extra cash. I think I will get a sack of crap boss, just that, a sack of crap for Boss's Day," Jason laughed as he quickly ended the call so as not to give Brice an opportunity to respond.

Jason entered the address for the Port of Laredo into his GPS and pulled onto the parkway towards and heading towards Interstate 55. He called Lindsey and placed the call on Bluetooth/hands-free to let her know he had been given new instructions on this current run and would be a couple more days before he arrived home. Lindsey as always was supportive and wished him safe journeys. Jason told her he loved her and to kiss the girls for him and that he missed them all.

CHAPTER 3

Port Laredo to Atlanta
to Port Laredo

Jason arrived mid-morning the next day at Port Laredo. He checked in through the guard shack and was directed to the nearest dock door to drop his container and pick up an empty trailer from their yard and deliver it to Staley's for loading. The process was a smooth one and Jason thought to himself what a relief it was to have a normal drop-and-hook opportunity at the port. He connected to his assigned empty container and pulled through the guard gate and began his drive to Atlanta and then home to his precious family. Jason was ready to be home and relax for a couple of days. Jason would need to stop for a driver clock reset somewhere between Louisiana and Mississippi and then he could be home by late afternoon the next day. He stopped at a rest stop on the Louisiana and Mississippi state line and as normal he had a cold can of soup, called Lindsey, and curled up in the sleeper compartment of his rig. The next morning, he awoke, grabbed a quick breakfast sandwich at the cafeteria located across from the rest stop, and showered quickly at the rest stop. He was ready to finish the remaining five hours or so of travel time to Atlanta. He fired his engine and slowly pulled onto the parkway. The traffic cooperated fully with Jason this sunny morning and he arrived at Staley's in roughly five hours.

He dropped his empty container in the yard and did not even feel like stepping in and speaking to Brice. He simply gave him a brief call to let him know he had arrived and would see him in two days if that was not going to be an issue. Brice assured Jason all was well and even offered to pay him for the two days due to the headaches he had experienced during this last run. Jason was thankful but again let Brice know it was not necessary and the extra day off would be payment enough.

Jason arrived home and crashed onto the sofa with his three favorite ladies. They spent the afternoon, and the evening curled up watching cartoons. Jason dozed in and out most of the time but held tightly to all three of his family. The next day the family visited Atlanta Zoo and had a day out together. They arrived home and Jason and Lindsey bathed the girls and got them ready for bed. Jason and Lindsey turned in early as they had not had a night to themselves in what felt like an eternity. The following morning and day were spent handling Jason's laundry and getting his cold lunches and dinners packed up for his next run.

Jason arrived at Staley's early the next morning and saw Brice's pickup truck in his parking spot in front of the main office. Jason already had his manifest for a return trip to Laredo from his dispatcher, but he wanted to say hello to Brice and see how he was doing. Jason made his way up the office steps and entered the main lobby. Kelly Parton was busy at her desk sending emails out to the drivers' dispatchers and receiving incoming calls from their customers. Kelly doubled as Brice's secretary and the customer complaint department most days. Jason walked by and tapped on her desk as she was busily taking notes from the current call which she was handling. He pointed towards Brice's office and smiled at her as he walked toward the corridor leading to the leadership offices. Kelly smiled and gave a quick wave of acknowledgement and focused back on her call and note taking. Jason paused in front of Brice's office and gently rapped on the door. Brice asked him to come in. Jason skipped inside and smiled at Brice as he stuck his hand out. Brice stuck his hand out and shook his friend's hand firmly and pointed to the chair across from his desk for Jason to sit down and he rounded his desk and plopped down in his leatherback desk chair. Jason sat down and smiled at his friend.

"What the hell are you doing here and not on some golf course squandering the hard-earned money we drivers are pouring in here for you. I nearly fainted when I saw someone other than Kelly's car in the parking lot when I arrived," Jason had to get the early punch in as he knew Brice was prepared for the first verbal, joking jab.

"Listen asshole. I was driving trucks and making miles when you were still pissing in your pants. I know that can be a bit misleading as I heard from Lindsey you were still pissing in your pants as recently as last week," Brice enjoyed the banter the two of them always seemed to experience.

"I am good my friend. I just wanted to stop in and say thanks for the extra day off and let you know that I am recharged and ready for the road."

"I am glad you got some well-deserved rest and my offer to pay for those two days still stands. I am glad you stopped by for another reason, also. I have some good news for you," Brice said. Brice leaned slightly forward and flipped over a couple of papers lying on his desk.

Jason spoke up before Brice could finish his thought. "So, you are going to retire, sell the business, and we can get some talented leadership in place here."

"You would not want that, Jason. The first thing anyone with half a brain would do is fire your ass and get someone in here who can put down some miles and make this operation successful. You better hope I live one day longer than you do so I can keep your ass employed." Brice laughed heartily and smiled back at Jason.

"Touche, boss. You got me, Jason couldn't help but admit that Brice had one upped him this particular occasion.

"Actually, my friend, Quinn Brown made the Windsor run the two days you were off and has brought back the container going to Laredo you have today. He said things were better in Windsor but still not a smooth operation by any stretch of the imagination. He is accustomed to the chaos up there and can deal with it better than you or I would. I think he has become numb to their idiocy. The fact that he is and was ok with the operation does not excuse the sloppy workmanship and I am going to continue to monitor the situation and make a decision about the long-term partnership in the coming months. Nonetheless, I can proudly say that you do not have to go to that piss-hole. I am going to ask our dispatchers to keep Quinn on that lane and save you other guys the headache. Do I get a hug?"

"Not if you were the last person on Earth and I was dying of diphtheria. I do appreciate the lane assignment and if Quinn is ok with that lane, then, let him run it damn it. This has made my day. I almost want to thank you, "Jason said with a smirk.

"Get on the road my friend and thanks for stopping in. I do appreciate your hard work and more than that your friendship. Be safe and I will see you in a few days."

Jason stood up and shook Brice's hand once more and wished him a good day and peaceful week. He exited the door and closed it quietly. He patted Kelly on the back as he walked back by her desk and smiled as she was obviously having a tough conversation with a customer on the line. He climbed down the steps, made his way to his rig, fired the engine, and hooked up to his container destined for Laredo. He almost danced a jig across the parking lot just now as he did not have to go to Windsor and maybe never again. He connected to his chassis, checked the load versus the manifest, and verified the locks. He was now on his way back to Laredo.

Jason crossed the Louisiana line and was roughly two hours away from the Port of Laredo. He heard a loud pop and smelled rubber burning. He knew he had a blowout on one of the chassis tires and would need to contact the roadside assistance team which

Staley's trucking had a contract. He called the roadside team after he had pulled onto the shoulder of the road and placed the fluorescent cones along the rear of the chassis and container. It was such a beautiful day he decided to get the sandwich Lindsey had made for him and have the sandwich and cup of coffee outside his rig. He grabbed the sandwich, poured a cup of coffee from his thermos, and stepped to the rear of the chassis to lean against the back of the container and await the roadside assistance technician.

As Jason stood in the sun enjoying his lunch, he noticed a small leak underneath the chassis which had come from the interior of the container. He looked underneath the container unit and observed a large water stain on the underside of the container. The container was locked down and Jason did not want to cut the lock without customer approval, but the leak was a concern for him. He ran up to the cab of his rig and quickly climbed inside. He grabbed the manifest from the passenger seat and speedily scanned the contents of the container listed on the document. Jason was a seasoned driver and knew what material was comprised of liquid and what material should have characteristics to produce leaks under heated conditions such as the inside of a transport container. He did a double run through of the manifest and confirmed there were no liquids or materials with liquid characteristics. He returned to the spot in which the liquid was slowly dripping, and Jason noticed an odd odor was emanating from the leak. Jason felt as if he knew what the odor was, but he was not taking any chances with what could become a contamination threat. He quickly called the roadside assistance team and asked them to dispatch a hazardous materials team member to assist in containing the spill and provide expert clean-up for the liquid spill. They could contact the DOT once the hazardous material personnel deemed necessary.

The hazardous material team member arrived before the roadside assistance team, parked behind Jason's container, and quickly grabbed their contamination test kit and the materials needed to secure the leak and treat it. When the person arrived at the front of the container where the leak was located and Jason was standing by to assist, he asked Jason how long it had been since he noticed the leaking substance. Jason explained it had been roughly thirty minutes and there was no more material leaking from the container. It had been fifteen to twenty minutes since any noticeable leaking had taken place. The hazardous materials personnel rapidly secured the five-foot perimeter around the material after having put on a portable respirator, protective gloves, and protective jumpsuit. Once the perimeter was secured with the proper absorbent padding, the gentlemen took a small swap and dapped it ever so carefully in the liquid. He placed the swap in a small test tube and stepped back over to his safety vehicle to test the liquid. It took less than three minutes for the test results to return. The gentlemen tossed the test tube into a hazardous waste container in the rear of his vehicle, removed the respirator, gloves, and jump suit and tossed them into the hazardous material container, also.

"Well, I don't think we need to be concerned with calling in extra specialists or anyone to clear up the spill. I think mother nature can handle it from here. By the way, my name is Gerald Spinks. I am sorry I didn't get to properly introduce myself when I arrived. I have been doing this line of work for twenty years and each call makes me as nervous as the first call I was ever dispatched twenty years ago. I feel as if I can never be cavalier about a roadside spill. I have seen some awful disasters and too many lives impacted when emergency personnel did not act quickly and correctly, "Gerald said as he wiped his hands with an antiseptic wipe and extended his hand to Jason.

"Mr. Spinks, I appreciate your quick response and professionalism. I can't imagine what you have seen over the years and safety for the environment and humans must be paramount. You mentioned that mother nature could clean this spill up. What did you mean by that? I had an idea what the liquid may have been, but I am no expert and was not about to take any chances, "Jason took Gerald's handshake and gently pulled him toward the edge of the road as he spotted the roadside assistance team humming up to them in their service truck.

"Please call me Gerald, Mr. Jennings. I had you at a disadvantage as my workorder listed your name and cell number. The liquid is human urine. It appears someone may have relieved themselves in the container and the leak was slow to make its way through the floor of the container. As luck would have it, your tire blowout must have shaken the urine off whatever the person loading the material whizzed on top of. It is a shame someone is too damn lazy to walk back inside a facility and use the restroom. What a world we live in," Gerald stood with a silly grin on his face and shook his head side to side in disbelief.

"Please call me Jason. That is odd. I will have to ask my boss to have his warehouse supervisors keep a closer eye on the loaders. Again, I appreciate the quick response and hope you have a good rest of your day."

Gerald began to gather up the absorbent pads he had placed around the leaking liquid now discovered to be human urine and place them in the hazardous material container in his service vehicle. Jason walked around the other side of the container to speak with the roadside assistance team who was replacing the blown-out chassis tire. Gerlad waved goodbye as he climbed back into his vehicle, fired the engine, and slowly pulled back onto the roadway. Jason stood and spoke with the roadside assistants as they did quick work of replacing the tire. They had Jason fitted with a new chassis tire and invoiced within thirty minutes. Jason thanked the two men and signed their invoice. As they loaded their repair equipment back into the service vehicle, Jason circled back around to the driver's side of his rig and climbed inside. He made a quick call to his wife and waited for the service team to finish loading their equipment and pull away. He cranked up the rig and pulled the gear into drive. He slowly pulled onto the roadway after confirming traffic was clear.

Jason pulled onto the interstate and used his voice command to have his cellular call, Brice. He quickly ended the call and murmured under his breath. He rode along in silence for the next few miles and replayed the information over and over in his mind to make sure he was not mistaken. No, he knew he was correct. This container was one that Quinn Brown had picked up from the Windsor facility and Staley's Logistics had not loaded this material. Jason thought to himself that those incompetent idiots could not only handle a basic load and unload of material, and now some of them were pissing in the rear of containers because they were too lazy and unconcerned to use a restroom like everyone else. Jason decided he would call Brice and let him know about the blowout so he would be expecting the invoice for the repair and that he would be late arriving at the Port of Laredo. He did decide he would wait until he arrived at the port to call and speak about yet another goof at the Windsor facility. Jason felt he may be complaining a little too often about Windsor, but something had to be done. He once again voice commanded his cellular to call Brice. Brice answered on the second ring and Jason explained about the blow out and his running late to Laredo. Brice teased him about costing the company more money than he was bringing in and told him to be safe. Brice would have the dispatcher reach out to Laredo and make them aware of the delay. Jason rolled along the interstate still thinking about the Windsor group pissing in a container versus using the restrooms. He hummed under his breath about them needing a good ass kicking.

Jason was about five miles outside the Port of Laredo and evening was beginning. He decided he would park at the truck stop convenience store nearby and go to sleep early and get an early start first thing in the morning. He pulled into a parking location and switched his rig off. He called his wife and told her he would be home in a couple of days. It was still early enough for him to give Brice a ring, also. Jason dialed the number and Brice answered as he most always does on the second ring.

'Listen here asshole. If you keep calling me, I am going to have to report you for stalking. Besides you're too ugly for me and not my type," Brice said. He wanted to get the first playful insult in before Jason could begin speaking.

"I wouldn't stalk your crazy ass if you were the last person on Earth. I'd rather die a cold and lonely death before I dealt with your stupidity day in and day out," Jason jabbed back not wanting to be outdone.

The two men laughed, and Jason spoke in a much more professional tone as he prepared to fill Brice in on the urination issue with the container he was carrying. "Look Brice, I know it seems I am a broken record on this entire Windsor facility and all their follies, but I thought you should know about something. While I was awaiting the service team to come out and replace the chassis blowout, I saw a liquid leaking from the underside of the container. I asked that a hazardous spill expert be sent out to contain and clean up the leak. When he arrived, he contained the leak and tested the liquid to verify what the nature of the leak consisted of. Unfortunately, it was human urine. I was going to let you know so you could speak with our warehouse supervisors and see if it was someone on our team. It dawned on me a few minutes later that this was a container from Windsor that Quinn had picked up and the container was locked there. It was some of that group again, buddy. I am sorry to keep harping on those guys, but they appear to need a complete rework and turnover in personnel there."

"I be damned. What the hell is wrong with that crew up there? I have had it, Jason. First thing in the morning, I am the head of operations there and telling them about the laundry list of crap we have had to endure there and now to top it all off, SOMEONE IS PISSING IN DAMN CONTAINERS," Brice was shouting and obviously was passed frustrated with the Windsor group.

"I hate to lose the business Brice, but I feel like we do need to get upper leadership involved and have them put in place some type of corrective actions. I am not convinced they may even know how poorly that facility is performing. One solid complaint from a customer like us may be just the leverage we need to cause a positive turnaround up there," Jason was attempting to lower the temperature a bit and keep Brice from canceling the relationship with the Windsor facility.

"I swear if this does not clear up the shenanigans there this time, we are done with those incompetent bozos. I mean it. They need to police some of this shit and get their act together. You get some rest buddy, and I will have an update for you when you call in the morning," Brice was cooling off but was still very frustrated.

"Thanks again, boss and you get some rest, as well." Jason ended the call and climbed into his sleeper compartment of the rig and drifted off to sleep.

He awoke the next morning before dawn and strolled over to the truck stop café for a shower and some breakfast. He told himself today was going to be a great day and he could be asleep beside his gorgeous wife and in his own bed tomorrow night, if all went well. He grabbed a hot shower and took a seat at the counter. He ordered an omelet and a cup of coffee. As he was enjoying his breakfast and reading the news on his phone, he saw the sun begin to peek over the horizon. He finished his breakfast, paid his bill, and headed for his rig. He was ready to get unloaded and head home to Georgia. He checked in with the guard at the main port entrance and was instructed to drive to the northernmost warehouse dock. He was greeted by a port associate when he arrived at the dock and was asked to drop the container in a holding location as it was not scheduled for immediate unloading. Jason was more than happy to comply because this meant he did not have to wait for a team to unload him. He could get his assigned container and be on the road home much more quickly. He found the parking location assigned for his container and he backed it into the spot. He lowered the fifth wheel and climbed outside of his rig to unhook the air hoses and chock the wheels. As he made his way around to unhook the air hoses, his heart sank. He saw what appeared to be water trickling from the rear of his rig and he thought to himself he was having radiator issues and would be down for repair and not get home tomorrow. He began to examine the source of the water and to his delight and surprise, the water was not from his radiator or rig but from the container. He chocked the wheels and decided the unhook from container so he and the port associate could examine the water more closely. He began to think that he may have acted rashly and maybe someone had not urinated in the container at Windsor, but he remembered that Gerald tested the liquid on the roadside and confirmed that it was human urine. He climbed back into his rig and pulled from underneath the chassis. Jason saw the port associate who had assisted him checking container numbers against a yard verification sheet and he motioned for the associate to come speak with him.

"Good morning. My name is Jason Jennings. I saw a water leak and initially thought it may be from my radiator, but it appears it must be coming from the container. There wasn't supposed to be any liquid materials in the container but perhaps there was an oversight on the manifest. I was hoping we could break the lock and have a look inside."

"Good morning, Mr. Jennings. My name is Raul Sanchez. Let's have a look at your manifest and double check for liquids. If there are none, I will radio my supervisor and let them know we need to break the lock and replace it with a new one afterwards."

The two men checked the manifest and there was no liquid material listed. Raul radioed his supervisor, explained the situation, and was given permission to break the lock and examine the contents for damage or leaks. Raul stepped over to his golf cart and retrieved a set of bolt cutters to remove the lock. He broke the lock and opened the two swinging doors. He and Jason climbed up into the container and were pleasantly surprised to find that they would be able to navigate the freight up to the front of the container with little issues, if need be. They began to check each pallet of material and could not find any leaks. The closer they got to the front of the container a strong odor began to permeate through the container. Jason looked at Raul and squinched his nose. He pointed to the front wall of the container and told Raul it smelled like urine. Raul shined his flashlight toward what he thought was the direction of the scent and waved the light back and forth over the front wall and materials along the front wall of the container. Just as he was about to turn and face Jason, he grabbed Raul and spun him around and had him direct his flashlight back along the front wall. The light fell upon four young girls who could not be more than fifteen or sixteen years old. They quickly attempted to hide behind a pallet of material as Jason jumped over the pallets in front of him to get to where the young girls were. He was constantly telling them not to be afraid and they were not going to hurt them and wanted to help them. The young girls were dirty, hungry, and very frightened as Jason and Raul motioned for them to walk to the rear of the trailer. Jason continued to speak to the girls, but they obviously did not understand him. One of the girls began to speak to the others and their native language was French. When they all arrived at the rear of the container, Raul jumped to the ground and extended a hand to the first of the young ladies. Jason walked up behind the one closest to Raul took her by the hand, smiled, and nodded for her to take Raul's hand with her free one. They were able to get all four girls on the ground beside Raul and Jason jumped to the ground beside him, also.

"Please call your supervisor and port security immediately," Jason said as calmly as he could to not demonstrate any emotion which might be perceived as hostile by the four girls.

Raul took a few steps away and grabbed the two-way radio from his belt. He called out for immediate security presence, emergency personnel to assist the four girls for any medical needs, and for his supervisor. The emergency medical team arrived in less than three minutes as they were escorted by the port security team who cleared the way of any port traffic and pedestrians along the route. The emergency team began to examine the four girls and escorted them to the ambulance for transport to the local hospital in Laredo. The local authorities would meet the girls there and investigate the issues surrounding their being locked in the transport container, but their health and welfare was the primary concern at this juncture. The security immediately locked down the area surrounding the container and placed two security officers on each side of the container to ensure no one entered or tampered with the container and its contents. Raul's supervisor arrived just a few minutes later and followed up with the security team and made sure they were in place. He then asked the chief security officer to follow Jason, Raul, and himself to the security office for a full report and investigation into the discovery of these four young ladies.

As they arrived at the parking lot in front of the security office, Jason, Raul's supervisor, and Raul stepped out of the vehicle driven by the supervisor and made their way up the steps leading to the office area. The chief security member was just a minute behind them and was entering the door moments after the three men made their way into the main conference room. He followed right behind them and took a seat at the head of the rectangular table in the center of the room. Just as he was about to introduce himself there was a loud knock at the door. The chief security team member rather abruptly barked at the person or persons on the other side to please go away and not to disturb them again. A voice from the other side spoke back quietly and informed them that the FBI had arrived and needed to speak with everyone involved in the incident this morning. The chief security member hurriedly leapt to his feet and opened the door. There were three people standing in the doorway. One was the petite secretary for the Port of Laredo security office and two people from the FBI. The security team member asked the secretary to show them on and asked the FBI members to have a seat. Once seated the security team member gently cleared his throat and spoke.

"My name is Luis Javo. I am the chief of security here at the Port of Laredo. The gentleman seated to my right is Raul Sanchez. He is the port team lead in charge of container operations. The person to his right is Mary Watson. She is the container operations supervisor. The gentleman to my left is Jason Jennings. He is the person who delivered the container this morning and was present when the four ladies were discovered," Mr. Javo spoke slowly, softly, and with a small crack in his voice.

"My name is Special Agent Jeff Wright with the FBI and my partner Special Agent Madison Wilkes. We need to see all manifests beginning with this container's origin and an account of every mile and stop associated with the container. Is everyone who was involved with this continue and the discovery of the four persons in this room now," Agent Wright asked with a very direct and authoritative tone.

"Yes sir. This is everyone. We have the container isolated and being guarded by port security now," Mr. Javo answered still obviously very nervous.

"The port security will be relieved shortly," Agent Wilkes interrupted Javo's next sentence.

"Relieved," Asked Javo inquisitively?

"Yes, relieved! The FBI is sending a team here to secure the area around the container and will handle all security related measures until we decide otherwise," Wilkes snapped back as she was visibly frustrated with Mr. Javo questioning their authority.

"Of course. Anyway we can be of assistance," Javo had lowered his tone even further.

Mr. Javo had his secretary bring in all documentation for the container which had carried the four young ladies. The secretary had been requesting information from the Windsor Warehouse and Staley Trucking. Jason had already turned over all the paperwork he had received and forwarded all emails to Mr. Javo to print for the agents that he had received from his dispatcher concerning his leg of the transportation of the container.

Agent Wilkes had taken Jason to a separate conference room to get all his information on the beginning of the trip and the stops he made along the way. Jason assured her the lock was never tampered with and he had not replaced it. Agent Wilkes spoke with Jason for over two hours and some of the questions were repetitive as she was hoping Jason may make an error in his detailing the events in case, he was making up information. Jason was honest and forthright with Agent Wilkes and his story matched each time she questioned him about the events. Agent Wilkes was satisfied with his responses and took down all of his personal information including his cell phone number, home address, and Brice's information at Staley Trucking. He was allowed to leave but would not take any container back to Staley Trucking. All containers in the Port of Laredo were going to be verified by the FBI and nothing would leave until all containers were verified. Jason returned to his rig and pulled toward the guard gate of the port. He was nervous, confused, and concerned all at once. He would stop by and see Brice when he arrived back in Atlanta and see if they could do some tracking on the container themselves.

CHAPTER 4

Jason and the Brunswick Meltdown

Jason arrived at Staley Trucking the next afternoon. He had stopped and completed his mandatory DOT rest requirement in Louisiana. He attempted to sleep but he could not do anything but toss and turn. He tried to eat a hamburger from the rest stop café there but was unable to eat as the four young ladies were constantly on his mind. He parked his rig and made his way into the main office at Staley. Brice was in his office and was expecting him. Jason walked past Kelly's desk focused headlong on Brice's office. Kelly spoke to Jason as he passed, and Jason managed to grunt "good morning" or something along those lines. He tapped rapidly on Brice's office door and did not wait to be asked to step inside. He walked quickly up to Brice's desk and sat down in the chair across from Brice.

"Brice, I am sorry to barge in here like this, but I want you to know first and foremost that I had no knowledge about those four girls inside that container. I want to begin tracking that container from the time it was built, if necessary, to find how in the hell they wound up inside of it and who is responsible for putting them inside of it," Jason had begun to shake, and his words were cracking as he tried to speak faster than his brain could process.

"I agree one hundred percent Jason. Please do not apologize about anything. I am as upset about this as you are. My reputation as a responsible and respectable business owner and human being is at stake here and I damn sure want to know every detail. I took most of the evening and arrived early this morning to gather every manifest and any other information I could gather surrounding the container in question. I don't care if I have to spend the next week doing nothing but reviewing this paper trail to find out who is responsible and what the hell is going on here," Brice looked determined and spoke with fire in his tone as he slammed the file full of documents down on his mahogany desktop.

"May I make copies of those, please? I would like to take a few days off. I need to relax and spend time with my girls. This has shaken me up pretty badly. I can't sleep. I close my eyes and all I see are those four girls and then I see my daughters' faces on their bodies. I promise to assist in reviewing but please let me stay home for a few days. I need to be with my family and hold them closer tonight." Jason had begun to tear up and his voice was shaking more and more as he was visibly shaken and emotionally impacted by the series of events these last few days.

Brice stood up and walked slowly over to Jason's chair and placed his hand on his shoulder. Jaason had begun the weep deeply and had placed his head in his hands as his elbows rested upon each of his knees. "My friend, you take as much time as you need. It will be paid time and before you say anything, I insist this be paid time. Please take a week and spend time with your beautiful family. I will ask Kelly to make copies and I will drop the documents off by your house when I leave this afternoon. Go home for now and relax, if you can," Brice said softly and compassionately as he hugged him.

Jason stood up and faced Brice. He Swung both arms around his friend and hugged him. He regained his composure, tried his tears with his handkerchief, and whispered "Thank you and I love you my friend".

He walked slowly to the door and glanced back at Brice and nodded his head gently toward his friend. Jason walked briskly down the hall and stopped by Kelly's desk to apologize for being what he felt was inexcusably rude to her when he arrived. Kelly smiled brightly at Jason and assured him no offence was taken. She touched his hand gently as to reassure him everything was going to be ok with the container incident and those four young women. Jason reached over to her desk and hugged her briefly and turned and exited the office. He climbed into his rig, fired the engine, and began his drive home. Jason was ready to see his wife and daughters and try to rest for a few days. Then it would be time to drill down on the paperwork associated with the container he transported to Laredo.

Jason pulled into the vacant lot where he always parked his rig and made his way along the sidewalk and up his driveway. He was met by all three of his ladies. April and Lauren out raced their mom to Jason and leapt into his awaiting arms. He squeezed the girls tightly and kissed them repeatedly as the thoughts of the last few days echoed in his mind. He set the girls down, one beside each of his legs, and Lindsey wrapped her arms tightly around his neck and kissed him passionately until the daughters began to make ewwwwwwwww noises at them. Jason smiled and told Lindsey he was thankful to be home and had a long story to tell her after dinner. The four of them walked into the house and each of them was wearing bright and beaming smiles. The troubles of the world wash away when Jason is in the presence of his family. He certainly needed this love today and would treasure this time with them.

Jason relaxed with his wife and daughters for the next two days. They spent time visiting the zoo, having a picnic in the park, and rollerblading throughout their neighborhood. The family time was full of laughter, mostly at Jason falling constantly as he attempted to stay erect underneath his rollerblades. This was just the recharge Jason needed after the incident in Laredo. As he lay in bed, he knew that tomorrow he would want to begin reviewing the manifests and paperwork associated with the container in which the young women were found. The news media had been covering the story, but little information was being made public at this point in the investigation.

He was still having nightmares about the women and could only picture his wife and daughters faces on the bodies. He gently kissed his wife on the cheek as she had drifted off to sleep as Jason stared into the darkness of their bedroom. She had lay there attentively listening to Jason describe the events in Laredo in full detail to her for over an hour. He knew she had seen information about the incident on the news and the internet and she knew it was a Staley's Trucking rig which had moved the container. She had a pretty good idea that it was Jason who had unknowingly transported the container and young women to the port. However, she wanted to allow Jason the opportunity to tell his story when he was prepared and in his own timeframe. Lindsey loved Jason wholeheartedly and knew he was struggling but also knew he would ask for her assistance and input when he needed it the most and she would be ready to support him unconditionally.

The next morning Jason had breakfast with his family and made his way to the upstairs guest bedroom which doubled as his office much of the time. He had locked the paperwork for the container in the filing cabinet located in the corner of the room closest to the door. He placed the papers on the rolltop desk situated next to the filing cabinet which was positioned in front of the bay windows overlooking his front yard. He smiled as he saw Lindsey and his daughters in the yard playing freeze tag and yelling in delight as they chased each other around the yard. Jason began to scrutinize the paperwork from its origin in Windsor until the time he delivered it to Laredo. He spent hours going back and forth over the paperwork looking for something, anything, that may point to why or how those women wound up inside of that container. Lindsey had come upstairs about thirty minutes earlier to see if he wanted to have lunch with her and the girls and Jason declined. He was focused and wanted to find answers. He was intently focused on these forms, and nothing would tear him away. Lindsey quietly opened the door once more and stood silently against the doorframe staring and smiling at Jason.

"Did you uncover anything in the paperwork?" Lindsey asked softly as she smiled and cocked her head slightly as she looked lovingly at her husband?

Absentmindedly responding and not looking up for more than a brief instant. "I am not hungry baby. I will come down for a late lunch in a bit. I just need to look over these forms for a few more minutes."

Lindsey began to laugh softly as she walked over to Jason's chair and rubbed the back of his neck gently. "Jason Jennings, if you don't come out of this bedroom/office in the next fifteen minutes, you will catch me sleeping on you again."

"What are you talking about, Lindsey? It can't be more than 2:00 PM or 2:30 PM. Are you going to take a nap?

Jason reached for his cell phone and tapped the screen so the time would display. "I'll be damned. It cannot be 11:00 PM. Lindsey, I am so sorry. I have missed the entire day with you and the girls."

"We knew you were focused when April and Lauren insisted on helping me set the table for dinner and we had more plates crash and break on the floor from their dropping them than those that actually made it on the table and we never heard you get up to check on the commotion." Lindsey had to laugh out loud at the story and Jason's blank look of how he could have worked through that sort of noise.

Jason slowly stood up from the desk and stretched his back. He gently reached out to his wife and pulled her into his chest. He rubbed her sandy blonde hair and told her loved her. He exhaled deeply and mumbled to her that it was time for bed. He would need to get back to work the next day. As he released his embrace, he reached over to the stack of paperwork he had on the desk and straightened those closest to him in a row. He and Lindsey smiled at each other and turned toward the door. As he reached for the door to open it for his wife, as he routinely did every door they walked through, Lindsey stopped and stared back at the desk and the paperwork Jason had just arranged. She slowly walked back towards the desk and began to visually scan the eight or nine pages closest to the desk chair Jason had been sitting in. He was curious as to what may have caught her eye and slowly began to walk towards her as she had now slid into the desk chair and was holding one particular document in her hand and placed it alongside the other seven pages in front of her. Jason asked what had caught her attention and she put her hand up as if to say hang tight one second. She continued to compare the document in her hand to the other documents directly in front of her.

"Does your office administrative team have an electric typewriter?" Lindsey asked Jason as she continued to stare at the paperwork.

With a small chuckle, Jason looked at her bewildered. "Kelly would have to Google what an electric typewriter was. She would think it was something the Pilgrims brought over on the *Mayflower* if she ever saw one. Why do you ask, baby? These documents are created via computer and printed on a very expensive laser printer. Kelly insisted on having a top-of-the-line printer to make the documents look extremely professional but everyone in the office knows she requested it because the printer toners are so simple to replace our girls could do it. She is very helpful and super smart but has a bit of a lazy streak," Jason's chuckle had become laughter at this point.

Lindsey reached out and grabbed Jason by the bottom of his shirt as he had turned to walk back towards the door to leave the room. "Wait a second, honey. Please look at this document and the difference in the other ones which belong to the same date, shipment, and packet of the load you took to Laredo. You must look closely. Grab a chair and pull it up here," Jason wasn't sure if that was optimism or concern in her voice. He walked over to the back of the room and pushed the extra office chair the girls mostly used as a fort for their indoor camping trips over to the desk beside Lindsey.

"Lindsey, I have looked at these documents all day and most of the night. I am not seeing anything."

Lindsey grabbed one of the documents on the desk with her left hand and positioned it beside the document she was holding in her right hand. "Look closely at the CTPAT lock number section on the document in my right hand and the document in my left hand. See the slight difference? This was carefully typed over with an electric typewriter. If you look very closely you can see there was a very, very thin line of white out applied. Whoever did this had to have a steady hand and a lot of dexterity to pull this off." Lindsey slowly placed both the documents back on the desk and turned and looked at Jason intently.

"Damn it baby. I knew those baby blue eyes were sexy as hell but look at you with that eagle-eyed vision. I wonder who could have changed the CTPAT lock number and more importantly, why. The question is why not just ask Kelly to recreate the manifest and re-enter the correct CTPAT lock number. She could have done this in a matter of less than a minute. You are the bomb, baby. I knew I married you for a reason. Not just for a smoking hot body and great cook. You are a brainy lady, too." Jason kissed his wife on the cheek as he hugged her tightly. "I am going to stop by first thing in the morning and talk to Brice about this and see if it helps uncover how those four ladies wound up in my container. Now, Mrs. Jennings, come to bed so I can reward my beautiful bride properly." Jason smiled and winked at Lindsey.

"No way. If you want to reward me, go to the kitchen, and wash the dinner dishes." Lindsey laughed at Jason as she raced out of the room and down the corridor to their bedroom.

Jason rose early the next morning. He quietly slipped into the girls' bedrooms and kissed them gently while they slept.

He gathered the paperwork from the desk and made his way towards the kitchen to fill his coffee thermos and say goodbye to Lindsey. Lindsey was already in the kitchen and had filled his thermos and wrapped up a bacon and egg sandwich in a paper towel for him to eat on the road. She knew he would want to be at Staley's before Brice arrived so he could see him first thing before the phones, emails, and clients took priority. Jason hugged his wife and told her he would call her as soon as he received his load to let her know where he was delivering and how long he would be gone. He would also update her on the conversation with Brice and see if her fine detective work would be the case cracking moment in this whole affair with the four French ladies.

Jason arrived at Staley's before anyone in the office and he took a seat on the banister of the steps leading up to the main entrance door to the office. Kelly arrived early as usual and unlocked the office door. She and Jason stepped inside, and she took her seat behind her desk. Jason knew the answer to his question, but he needed to ask anyway. He let Kelly get settled in and make her a cup of coffee from the Keurig machine. Kelly liked things quick and efficient that is why he knew she would know nothing about an electric typewriter nor desire to own and operate one. She asked Jason if he wanted a cup, and he shook his head no. She grabbed her coffee and made her way to her desk.

"So, what's up, Jason? Why are you here so early? I thought you would take a couple more days off and try to relax from the incident in Texas. I know you had nothing to do with it and it had to be a severe shock for you. Brice and everyone in the office has been so worried about those four young women and you, also. How are you holding up?"

"Thanks Kelly. I appreciate your asking, and I am really good. I am just concerned for those young women, and I had a couple of things I needed to cover with Brice and wanted to catch him before the daily chaos began for him. Do you have a couple of minutes? I know you are busy and keeping Brice organized is a chore in and of itself, but I wanted to ask you something."

"For you, anything Jason." Kelly smiled brightly and reached over and took her telephone receiver out of the cradle so it would not ring and interrupt their conversation.

"Do you have or know anyone in the office who has an electric typewriter?"

"Jason, even if I had one, I would have to watch a YouTube video on how to begin to operate a dinosaur like that. Let me think. It seems as if I have seen one here before, but I can't say with certainty if it was at this office or even if I saw someone here using one. Why do you ask?"

"It is a long story. So, I was checking on," before Jason could finish his sentence the front office door opened, and Brice came walking through.

"Good morning sunshine. You are up early and in the office before noon. The wife must have run you away from home or all the golf courses must be closed for ground keeping," Jason smirked as he extended his hand toward Brice.

"Listen smart ass. Someone must get here and make money. I am barely scrapping by and may have to file bankruptcy soon," Brice grabbed Jason's hand, smiled at him, and shook his friend's hand.

Jason spun back around to Kelly and said thank you and that he would talk with her later. Then he followed Brice into his office and sat down.

"What is on your mind my friend? More importantly why are you back so soon? You will be paid for the time you are away. You know that. That had to be quite an ordeal for you down in Texas and you take all the time you need," Brice said. Reassuring his old friend that he was in his corner and here to support his time away from work.

"I am good, Brice. Really, I am. I did want to mention something to you, and I must confess, it was Lindsey who spotted it. I went over those documents for hours and hours yesterday trying to find some clue as to how and when those four women were loaded into the container I was delivering. I could not find any clue whatsoever. I looked over everything hoping one small detail would leap out at me and help us uncover the mystery behind this. Lindsey started scouring over the documents. She showed me where someone had changed the CTPAT lock number on the document and used white out and of all things, an electric typewriter to make the changes. I was asking Kelly if she had one and we all know the answer to that. She told me she didn't recall anyone here having one. I know it is a long shot, but do you know anyone here who has one and why would someone be so secretive about changing the lock number or am I being paranoid?" Jason seemed to be talking to himself more than Brice and desperately searching for absolution.

"Jason, I don't know of anyone who has an electric typewriter here and you are not paranoid. You are searching for answers, as we all are, and I appreciate the effort. I have been reviewing those same documents. I know you have the originals, and we made several copies for the FBI, several for our office, Laredo, and Windsor to review and assist in finding answers. Let me do some digging and see what I can unearth on my end, and I will call you immediately once I have some answers. Tell Lindsey great detective work and she may need to become a private investigator once the girls are both in school. Shifting gears for just a second, I wasn't expecting you back this morning to be honest and I did not ask our dispatcher team to assign a delivery for you. Can you give me thirty minutes to an hour to contact them and get you going, if you feel up to it?"

Jason agreed to wait as he really wanted to get back into a semi-normal routine again. He knew he would never be truly one hundred percent at peace until the matter in Laredo was resolved. He stepped out and walked down to the break room to get a cup of coffee and a snack. Brice agreed to get him rolling as soon as possible in the next hour.

Brice, true to his word, came down to the breakroom where Jason was now surfing the internet on his cell phone. He motioned for him to come into the corridor and grab his paperwork for the pending delivery. Brice handed over the paperwork neatly housed in a manilla folder and shook Jason's hand. He asked that he be safe and would call him with any updates. Jason looked at the paperwork and looked back up at Brice.

"Thank you, Brice. This is a great delivery. I get to travel down to Brunswick. That will be a quick turn, and I can get home and maybe have time to call Ronald Watts and see if he can have lunch.

"Jason, one more minute please. Can you hang around the breakroom for a few more minutes? I need to check on an invoice we received down in my office. I may need you to verify some information so I can get Kelly to push it through accounting for payment. "

"Absolutely. I will have myself a second cup of coffee if you promise not to tell Lindsey. She thinks one cup in the morning is all I need." Jason smiled broadly as he walked over to the coffee maker.

Brice came back into the breakroom about fifteen minutes later looking a severely disheveled. He walked right past Jason where he was now sitting and playing a card game on his cell phone. He walked quickly over to the coffee maker and poured himself a cup of coffee but spilled more on the floor than he seemed to fill his cup. He murmured a profanity under his breath and pulled several paper towels from the dispenser and began to wipe up the coffee spill. Jason walked over and knelt beside him and began to help him clean up the spill.

"What are you still doing here? I thought you were on your way to Brunswick with the container we assigned to you," Brice nervously wiped up the remaining coffee spill and both men rose to their feet.

"Brice, are you ok? You asked me to stay in the breakroom while you went to check on an invoice that you may have needed me to review. You look like you saw a damn ghost man," Jason said reaching out and touching him on the shoulder.

"Oh yes. Yes….I'm good. I just received a call from an angry client. Apparently one of the drivers damaged some merchandise in transit and they were reading the riot act demanding we pay for the damaged material. Don't worry about that invoice. I will try to find it. I don't want to hold you up any longer. Get in the road and if you see Ronald tell him I said hello." Brice was still shaking somewhat but seemed to be coming back down to Earth.

"Hey, don't let one frustrated customer ruin your entire day boss. You have seen these types of situations before, and they always cool down and keep doing business with us. We are the best firm in the Southeast and everyone knows it."

Jason walked out of the office building and towards his rig. He would be on the road soon and hopefully see his friend and maybe, if the delivery location went smoothly, he could be back home before his girls went to bed and could kiss them good night. He fired up the engine and backed underneath his assigned trailer and slowly pulled out of the Staley's Trucking lot. The traffic on Interstate 95 was moving well, once he was out of the chaotic metro Atlanta traffic. He had rolled down the driver's side window of his rig and was enjoying the cool breeze as it blew through his hair. It only seemed like a few minutes when he saw his exit number twenty-eight was only seven more miles. He had to pull through the weigh station on the outskirts of Brunswick to ensure he was within the DOT required weight regulations. Jason decided while he was on the scales he would quickly call Ronald and see if he could break away for not only lunch but maybe a quick ride over the Sidney Lanier Bridge onto Jekyll Island and he could pick up a few seashells for his daughters. They were making themselves a Hollywood starlet necklace with the shells. That's what April and Lauren called the work in progress jewelry accessory anyway.

Jason pulled onto the scale when it was his turn and pulled out his cell phone to call Ronald. He had no sooner located

Ronald's number in his contact list and was about to place the call when he saw the DOT inspector quickly open the scale office door and swiftly begin to walk towards his rig. Jason placed the cell phone back into the pocket of his red flannel shirt and waited for the DOT officer to explain what he needed.

"Sir, please step down from the rig. I need to see your CDL licenses, manifest, and I will need you to open the trailer doors immediately." The officer was firm in his tone and Jason could sense that he was suspicious of something or there was an issue with the weight of the container.

"Is there a problem with the weight limit Officer Cribb?" Jason had seen the officer's name was Jeremy Cribb from the DOT badge pinned to his officer's uniform.

"Sir, please let me see your CDL license, manifest, and come to the rear of the container and open it immediately." Officer Cribb was now much sterner, and his voice was hardening and rising with each word of the request.

"Yes sir, of course. I am sorry if I seem uncooperative, but I am just a little confused about what the underlying issue may be." He was apologetic and handed the license and manifest to the officer as he quickly made his way to the rear of the trailer with the officer literally stride for stride beside him as they walked.

Jason cut the lock and swung the doors open. As he was stepping aside to allow Officer Cribb to perform his inspection a siren in the distance caught his attention as a patrol car raced up the DOT inspection exit. The patrol car was followed by a DOT inspection patrol car and two other Sheriff's cars as they raced up the exit toward them with lights blazing and all sirens blaring. As the lead vehicle approached the rig, Jason saw it was his friend, Sheriff Ronald Watts. A feeling of relief fell over Jason as he knew Ronald would shed some light on the issue at hand and he was thrilled to see a friendly face as Officer Cribb looked very perturbed.

"Ronald, it is good to see you my friend," Jason said with a smile as he stuck his hand out to greet his old friend.

"Jason Jennings, please step to the side of the patrol car and do not move from that spot until instructed," Ronald did not extend his hand in return and was completely by the book and very authoritative in his remarks.

"Ronald what is going on here?" Jason had now been grabbed on his bicep by one of the deputies and pulled to the car Ronald had pointed at just a moment ago.

The deputy stood by Jason and the remaining deputies and DOT officer who arrived were now huddling around the patrol car along with Jason. They shifted their focus between Jason and the now open container which Jason was transporting. Officer Cribb and Ronald had conducted a search of the cab of the rig and had now disappeared inside the container. They were inside the container for what felt like an eternity as far as Jason was concerned but resurfaced on the ground about ten minutes after entering it. Jason saw Ronald carrying a small black case no larger than a shaving kit as he leapt down from inside the container. Jason recognized the case as one where he kept some personal hygiene items inside and locked inside his locker in the shower room at Staley's Trucking. He kept it there in case he wanted to brush his teeth or shave a three-day old beard before he traveled home after a stretch on the road. He was thinking how in the hell did it wind up in the back of this container.

"Mr. Jennings, is this your bag?" Ronald questioned Jason, looking intently at him then at the black bag.

"Yes, it's mine. I kept it in my locker at Staley's so I could freshen up there before I go home sometimes. I have no idea how it got into this container. I haven't used any of the contents for several weeks. This is crazy. What does a shaving kit have to do with all this commotion?"

"We received an anonymous tip from someone saying they were employed at Staley's Trucking and that they suspected you of transporting drugs inside your containers. They went on to say they saw you toss this bag into your container before you departed this morning. We have found what appears to be nearly four kilograms of cocaine inside. We need you to turn around and place your hands on the car. Deputy, please read Mr. Jennings his rights and place him under arrest," Ronald never wavered in his duties, but he was painfully sorry to have to place his old friend under arrest.

"Wait just a damn minute, Ronald, you know I am not a drug trafficker. I have been set up. For God's sake man, LISTEN TO ME! This is ridiculous, Jason had not spun around quickly enough, and the deputy had snatched his left arm behind his back and shoved him furiously on the hood of Ronald's patrol car. Jason's hat flew off and hit the ground and he struggled to turn around and face Ronald to speak with him. Each time he attempted to spin around; the deputy would more forcefully shove him back onto the hood of the car. Ronald walked away as the deputy finished reading Jason his rights and placed him in the back of the patrol car. Jason sat bewildered and handcuffed in the back of the patrol car and watched Ronald pull onto the interstate. He looked back to see Officer Cribb slowly pulling his rig into a parking spot adjacent to the weigh station office. He could not believe his friend had just had him handcuffed and arrested without hearing his side of the story.

CHAPTER 5

Ronald and Jason
Discuss the Arrest

Jason was booked, mugshot taken, and fingerprinted before he was moved to a holding cell. After forty-five minutes, Jason looked up from the steel bed he was sitting on with his head buried in his hands. An officer instructed Jason to step forward once he opened the cell door. Jason stood up as asked and walked slowly toward the officer. The officer grabbed him by the right arm and gently shoved him into the corridor toward what appeared to be the front of the Sheriff's Office. As they reached another set of locked doors the officer called out to another officer located in the control room and asked him to unlock the door for interrogation. A loud buzzer sounded as the control room officer opened the door as asked and the officer once again grabbed Jason by the right arm and tugged him through the cell doorway.

They walked roughly twenty-five yards and the officer instructed Jason to stand by another doorway as he unlocked interrogation room two. Once unlocked, the officer opened the door and instructed Jason to step inside, have a seat, and do not move until someone from the Sheriff's Office instructed him to do so. Jason swiftly stepped inside, went directly to an open wooden chair located underneath a small, rectangular, wooden table, and sat down. He kept his hands in plain view as the officer closed the door and Jason heard him place a key in the door and lock it. There was no clock inside the interrogation room, so Jason had no idea how long he had been sitting alone inside the locked room. It felt like hours. Just as he had begun to think someone had forgotten about him, he heard a set of footsteps outside in the corridor and seconds later a key in the lock of the door. Jason thought they were simply preparing a spot for him in the general population area and were now coming to retrieve him and take him to his cell. The door swung open and Sheriff Watts, Jason's oldest friend, was standing in the doorway. Ronald pulled the door closed behind him, locked, and walked over to the window facing the opposite side of the interrogation room. He slowly closed the Venetian Blinds to completely cover the view into the room and turned to face his old friend.

"Jason, I am so sorry for the formality back at the weigh station, but I have a duty and obligation to serve law and justice despite my personal feelings. I do not want you to think in any way that I believe you are running drugs. I do, however, must execute the same procedures for this type of arrest for everyone. Even though I love them and believe in their innocence completely," Sheriff Watts said, with a crack in his voice. Ronald walked over to his friend, sat down beside him, and threw his arms around him, and hugged him heartily.

"Thank you, my friend. I am innocent of this and have no damn idea how those drugs got into that container. I am not a drug runner, Ronald. I have been set up and I don't know why," Jason said still hanging on to his friend's embrace and had begun to cry slightly.

Ronald sat back into the chair closest to his friend and took a deep breath. "I want you to start at the beginning and tell me everything you did this morning until you arrived at the weigh station. I need you to start from the time you woke up this morning until the weigh station incident when I arrived. Do not leave anything out despite how trivial you think it may be.

I want everyone you spoke with and every step you took today retraced. I know you are not a drug runner, and we are going to find out who is responsible for this setup." Ronald's sad demeanor had quickly turned to a stern look of determination and obvious anger over this incident and was prepared to assist his friend in every way possible.

Jason inched forward into his chair and placed his hands on the table and cupped them together. He shuffled in his seat slightly and looked Ronald directly in the eyes as he began to detail each moment of his morning to Ronald beginning with his waking up at home and every moment until he arrived at the weigh station. His details were distinct, and Jason did not leave any detail untold. He accounted for every minute of his day up to his arrival at the weigh station.

Ronald had taken his cell phone out of his pocket and was recording the entirety of the conversation. He had also picked up a legal pad and pen which had been sitting on the wooden desk and was making notes of questions he wanted to ask once Jason was finished speaking and potential theories he may have as to where the drugs came from. Once Jason had detailed everything up to the arrest at the weigh station, Ronald turned off the recording on the cell phone and placed the pen atop the legal pad he had been writing on.

"Ok, Jason. Who would want to do you any harm or set you up for some kind of a fall like this? I know you are friendly to everyone, and I can't imagine you having any enemies, but I need you to think. Have you had any type of disagreement with anyone at Staley's Trucking? Have you had a disagreement with a co-worker, a neighbor, or a customer? I know about the incident in Laredo. The FBI has been in touch with me and kept me abreast of the developments in the case. They have completely removed you from suspicion and I assured them you had no knowledge of what happened with those four women in that container. Someone, and I hate to say it, probably at Staley's has some sort of axe to grind with you and is trying to get you paid back and paid back big time."

"No one, Ronald. I mean, no one. I don't cross anyone, and I barely do anything outside of work without Lindsey and the girls. I haven't had a cross-word with anyone. I was upset about the lack of professionalism at the Windsor facility and spoke with Brice about it but I was never ugly to anyone at the facility nor did I elevate it to anyone at Windsor. I looked over some paperwork and Lindsey actually saw where a CTPAT lock number had been modified. I spoke with Brice about it and he said he would look into it. Brice has been as upset about the Laredo thing as I have and has been checking on things on his own as he cooperates with the FBI. Can I ask a question off the record? Whose number was associated with the anonymous tip your office received from Staley's Trucking? I am sure you have already investigated that, and I am sure that can go a long way into explaining what the hell is going on here.

"I can get into a ton of trouble here, Jason. Please, please tread lightly with this information. The call came in on a burner cell phone. The call was not from Staley's location but was within a three-mile radius of Staley's address. This means someone could have pretended to be Staley's employee or could have been an employee and simply driven a few miles from the business and made the call. How many people work there and how soon can we check the video from his cameras to see who may have exited the grounds and could have made the call?"

"Ronald, there must be seventy-five to eighty associates there. This includes everyone from Brice to drivers to office staff to custodians. I have never angered anyone there and not sure why anyone would want to implicate me in something like this. As soon as I can post bail, we will call Brice and head back to Atlanta immediately to review the videos."

"Bail is not possible, Jason."

"What the hell man. You cannot be seriously thinking of not allowing me to post bail. I am not a flight risk. You must help me, Ronald." Jason said. Desperation and disbelief had begun to resonate from his voice as he interrupted Ronald's sentence.

"Let me finish my friend. Bail is not needed because I have called my old friend Judge Russell Everett. After I turned on the old Watts' charm, Judge Everett decided to release you on your own recognizance and I would be responsible for your return for a trial date, once on the docket.

"The old Watts' charm huh? How about Watts being full of BS? That sounds much more accurate. I do not know how to repay you. I want to clear my name and find out who is behind all of this. I am going home now and will meet you at Staley's first thing in the morning. I need to get my cell phone, please, so I can locate an UBER ride home," Jason now had a small tear racing down the side of his cheek as he hugged his friend tightly once again.

"No need for the UBER. I will take you home and stay the night, if Lindsey promises to make some or her world-famous fried chicken and potatoes for dinner." We can both get up first thing and arrive at Staley's to meet Brice and review the video.

The two men walked out of the Sheriff's Office immediately after Jason had retrieved his personal effects from the property room. The two men had a lot to talk about on the four-hour drive to suburban Atlanta. Jason had over twenty missed calls from Lindsey and Brice. He called Lindsey first and reassured her that everything was alright and that he would fill her in on all the events of the day when he arrived home. He also let her know to set one extra spot for dinner tonight. Ronald wanted his fried chicken. He called Brice and told him the same story. For some reason, Jason was a bit guarded about the events and Ronald being with him. Jason had not verbalized this yet, but he was not sure what role, if any, his friend and boss was playing in this saga and in his own heart, Jason felt that he may be the one who set him up. He did not know why but the nagging feeling would not leave his gut. Jason's dad always told him to trust his gut and more times than not your gut instinct would prove true. He certainly hoped he was wrong this time, but the thoughts still lingered. Jason and Ronald rode and talked about today and more about all their yesterdays. Jason was glad to have his friend with him and knew he would be by his side until the real criminals were brought to justice. They had run a gamut of emotions today and as the miles clicked away and Jason's home got closer and closer the two men had no idea the peril and frustration that awaited them in the upcoming days and weeks.

CHAPTER 6

An Instinct and a Clue

Jason, Ronald, and Lindsey sat down to a late dinner. The girls had already been put to bed before the guys arrived home from Brunswick. As requested, Lindsey had made her delicious fried chicken, potatoes, and even had time to toss an apple pie in the oven for dessert. The three friends sat and ate and discussed what had transpired earlier in the day. Lindsey was concerned for Jason but he and Ronald Assured her that everything would soon be solved, and justice served. Ronald had begun to help Lindsey clear the table and Jason remarked that they had been talking for over three hours and it was now after midnight. Lindsey told Ronald to grab a shower and that the guest room had been made up for him. She told Jason to grab a shower and head to bed, also. She would finish clearing the table and putting everything away. She would handle the dishes tomorrow morning after breakfast. The men agreed to meet downstairs for a quick cup of coffee and some bacon for breakfast at 6:00 AM and then leave immediately for Staley's Trucking. They had a full day planned there and needed to get an early start. Jason kissed his wife and thanked his friend once again. Ronald thanked Lindsey for the outstanding meal and conversation, and he too headed for a shower and bed. Jason, of course, could not turn in until he had slipped into the girls' bedrooms and kissed them goodnight.

The next morning the to men met in the kitchen. Lindsey already had the kitchen smelling of fresh brewed coffee, hickory bacon, and sweet blueberry muffins. The three of them sat down and enjoyed a quick breakfast and Jason and Ronald headed for Ronald's cruiser. They were on the road by 6:40 AM and should be at Staley's by no later than 7:30 AM. The suburban traffic cooperated for once and the two men arrived at Staley's at exactly 7:30 AM. The only car in the parking lot, as expected, was Kelly Parton's. The two men entered the main office door, spoke to Kelly, and told her they needed to use Brice's office until he arrived. She smiled brightly and told them to make themselves at home. She turned back to her work she had begun on her desktop computer and the two men made their way down the hallway to Brice's office and let themselves in. They sat down at a small mahogany table. The two men spread out their paperwork and began to intently scan the copies and notes they had each made the night before. Jason's notes were more detailed as he had begun to make notes on them the day Lindsey had some observantly noticed the typewritten change on one of the documents. Ronald and Jason were so engrossed in their notes that they did not hear the office door swing open nor did they see Brice quietly walk over to where the two men had their heads buried in the paperwork. Brice stood there between the two for almost 45 seconds when he finally touched Jason on the shoulder to let him know he was in the room. Jason was so preoccupied with his notes and the questions swirling in his head he literally lifted himself up slightly in his chair and gave out a yelp as if he were a dog suddenly popped with a switch. He cursed under his breath as he settled back into his chair and tapped his chest in an attempt to stop his heart from beating out of his shirt. When he finally regained his composure, he looked up at Brice and pointed to Ronald to try and communicate an introduction.

"Geez man. You scared the hell out of me. I might need to go and see if I need a change of underpants and jeans. How long have you been standing there? I guess neither one of us heard you enter.

You damn near gave me a heart attack. "Jason was slowly catching his breath and managing a small smile as he was still clutching his chest.

"I saw you two guys and it looked like you were both in a different world. I am sorry I startled you guys. I am so sorry for this entire ugly mess. I know you had nothing to do with any drugs and drug movement. Ronald, it has been a long time. I am not sure if you remember me, but I saw you and your girlfriend at one of the company's picnics a few years back. Jason has spoken so often about you and so highly of you I wanted to meet you. I only had time to shake your hand and briefly say hello. I wish our second meeting now was under a more festive occasion. I am thrilled that you are here to support Jason and help apprehend and convict the true guilty party," Brice extended his hand toward Ronald as Ronald stood up to shake his hand and greet Brice properly.

"Thank you for opening your shop and office to us. I know you are extremely busy and have a lot of balls in the air. I, we, will try to be brief but anything you can do would be huge in putting this entire mystery together. I know you feel as strongly as I do about Jason's innocence. He is ugly as hell, so we need to make sure we don't add any more undo pressure on him. The only thing he has going for him is his gorgeous wife and children and God only knows why they stick around," Ronald said trying to lighten the mood a bit and help grease the wheels for what promised to be a difficult discussion.

Brice sat down in the empty chair beside Jason and looked at both men with a countenance of concern and apathy. He reached over to an office phone hanging on the wall to the right of him and it buzzed to the front desk where Kelly was sitting. Brice asked her to reschedule any appointments for today and take messages on all incoming calls for him for today. He mentioned that he may need her to order lunch later and have it delivered for the three of them but would let her know shortly. He swiftly hung the phone up and returned his focus to Ronald and Jason.

"I just needed to ensure we had no interruptions, and my day was clear to help in any way I can. If this discussion carries over into tomorrow, then I will clear tomorrow's schedule as well. There is nothing and I do mean nothing more important to me right now than to prove that this honest and upright man is proven innocent and cleared of all charges. There is not much I can do about his ragged and unsightly appearance. It seems as if Mother Nature was seeking revenge on him for some wrong, he did as a child."

"You guys are a couple of asses. But I am glad you are my asses. I need all the friends I can get right now. I keep up a brave façade for Lindsey because I do not want her to worry but guys, I don't see how this could look any worse for me. I have tried to think of someone, anyone, who would want to frame me for something like this, but I do not have any enemies that would want to set me up this way. I am sure I have pissed off some customers and maybe even a couple of coworkers at some point but nothing so severe to plant drugs on me," Jason said. His voice had begun to crack as he felt this unwarranted betrayal crashing down inside of himself.

"We are going to solve this mystery and apprehend the correct person or persons, Jason. You have my word as your friend and law officer. You can take that to the bank. Besides, I need you to hang out with me on the beaches of Jekyll Island and St. Simons to keep up my reputation as Ronald the sex god," Ronald smiled brightly at his friend and touched his shoulder gently in a firm attempt to reassure him of the support he was going to receive and take one last jab at lightening the mood before the questions began.

Both Ronald and Jason took turns sharing their copies of the packing lists and explaining their notes to Brice. The morning rolled into the noon hour and Kelly quietly slipped inside the office and brought the three men some Chinese she had ordered for lunch. She placed the plates and three bottles of water on the now vacant mahogany table as all three were now walking about the office as they discussed the information and reviewed the copies of the paperwork. Kelly smiled brightly and waved as she quietly slipped back out of the office and went down the corridor to her desk. The three men sat down in front of their Styrofoam plates and silently ate their lunch. The three had sporks in one hand and paperwork in the other as they refused to stop their thought processes even for a meal. Finally, Ronald stood up and insisted the three of them step outside for some fresh air and a ten-minute break from their internal investigation. Brice and Jason both agreed a break was long overdue and a few minutes of downtime may prove beneficial for their search. They were all three unsure of what they were looking for and Jason and Ronald were hoping and praying they could avoid asking Brice some very poignant questions they both knew would make him feel uneasy. Neither of them wanted it to go there but each of them knew as the time wore on and answers did not come in, that these questions would have to be asked. If these questions proved to be another dead-end, then Brice would surely be insulted and maybe even ruin a friendship he and Jason had enjoyed for years. Jason and Ronald, however, were willing to go down that road but just extremely begrudgingly.

The break was certainly well needed, and the three men gathered back inside of Brice's office after a ten-to-fifteen-minute break for the restroom and a quick walk outside to momentarily clear their heads and take in the crisp afternoon and, fresh air. Brice sat on the edge of his desk and looked out at Ronald and Jason as they circled the mahogany desk with their faces still buried in the paperwork. It seemed like hours, but it was about two minutes when Ronald stopped walking. Jason did not notice that Ronald had stopped moving as he was so engrossed in his paperwork and notes, that he bumped into Ronald and nearly knocked him over.

Ronald pulled up a chair from underneath the table and sat down. He took a deep breath and looked at Brice and then again at Jason. "Guys, I hate to do this, but I need to check in with my office. It is almost 2:00 PM and I have not spoken to anyone there today. I'm sure all is well there but I do need to check in with my deputies on duty. If you guys want to stay and discuss the paperwork, I can regroup with you all in an hour or so."

Jason looked up from his paperwork and then glanced at Ronald and Brice. "Let's call it a day and meet back first thing in the morning. I have texts from Lindsey I have not had the opportunity to answer, and Brice has calls, emails, and messages he needs to follow up on. We have spent a lot of time and covered a lot of ground today. Maybe a break for the afternoon and some downtime will help jar something loose. We all need a break. Brice, I need to use some of my vacation time until this all blows over to ensure I have a paycheck coming in. The bills keep coming and if I must hire an attorney, I am sure the retainer fee will be huge."

"Guys, I have cleared my schedule and will keep it clear for as many days as needed. There are no business transactions more important to me than seeing Jason cleared of all the charges here. As far as vacation time is concerned, you will not burn it on this. You save it and take your girls on a vacation when this is all over. You are on the clock and will be paid regularly. Furthermore, if you need an attorney, Staley's Trucking will pay the retainer fee and their fee, as needed. You are innocent and this company will back you to prove it," Brice walked over and hugged Jason as he spoke.

"Brice, I am grateful. I am going to head home and spend some time with the girls. Ronald, call me later and let me know what time you would like to meet back here tomorrow morning. I will take a UBER this afternoon and will use Lindsey's car tomorrow to meet everyone here. Ronald, if you can stay the night, let me know when you call, and we will set an extra place for dinner tonight."

"I will be staying tonight and stay until we have some concrete answers and resolution. Please ask Lindsey not to go to any extra trouble for dinner. Her normal five course meal will suffice and tell her I like strawberry cheesecake for dessert tonight," Ronald winked at Jason and shook Brice's hand as he opened the office door and slipped down the corridor.

Jason smiled at Brice and opened the door himself and he too made his way down the corridor to the front door. He stopped by and thanked Kelly for the lunch and asked if he could pay for the meals. She looked at him in bewilderment, winked at him, and laughed as she explained that she used office petty cash for the lunches and even bought herself some lunch but asked Jason not to tell Brice. Jason managed a small laugh and thanked her again.

Jason's UBER arrived about twenty minutes later. He slid into the backseat of the jet-black Hyundai Sonata and greeted the UBER driver. The young woman driving made small talk with Jason as is customary for most UBER drivers as they hope to influence a larger tip and it helps pass the time as the miles click by during the ride. The ride took about forty-five minutes as Atlanta afternoon traffic was beginning to kick off for the day. The UBER ride pulled up in Jason's driveway around 4:00 PM. He thanked the driver and climbed out of the backseat. He was beginning the walk up the driveway when Ronald's cruiser came gliding up behind him. Jason finished rating the driver and providing a tip for the driver on the app and looked up and smiled at Ronald as he put the car in park and turned off the engine. Ronald almost jumped out of the driver's seat and jogged up to Jason. He also quickly sent a text to Lindsey and let her know they would be outside for a few minutes discussing what transpired today and he would fill her in after dinner. He asked her to keep the girls inside until he and Ronald were finished and could come inside.

"So, what did you think was so important that you had to give me our exit buzzwords back there in Brice's office. I hope it is something good and can shed some light on the case," Jason was looking at Ronald with anticipation hoping and praying for good news.

"I am so glad we discussed an exit phrase this morning on the drive into Staley's. I would have hated for you to stand there another several hours or think I had placed greater importance on some other type of work ahead of our mission. I did need to get us out of there as I saw something that may or may not be pivotal, but I needed to talk with you when Brice was not present. I am still not 100%

convinced he is our guy, but I need to speak with you about what I saw and get your thoughts. I don't want it to be him but rather be safe than sorry."

"You always think of everything. You have been thinking of ways to get us out of conversations or predicaments since we were teenagers. You should have been a double agent or an attorney instead of a sheriff," Jason winked at Ronald as he focused his full attention on his friend's every word.

"Listen here, buddy. You can call me a double agent or a bootlegger, or any other foul creature, but don't you ever compare me to attorney ever again or this friendship has come to an ugly end. "

"Understood, esquire. I mean Sheriff Watts," Jason laughed out loud for the first time in days, and it honestly felt therapeutic.

"Here goes. While we were having our little break. I slipped back inside while you guys were outside talking. If you recall, I excused myself for a quick trip to the restroom. Actually, I wanted to slip back into Brice's office and look around. What was I looking for? I truly don't know. I want to eliminate Brice as a suspect because he is your friend, and I don't like to think he would set you up for any reason. At this point, I can't afford to cross anyone off the list from Staley's office until I am completely certain they were and are not involved. I went to Brice's office and started looking through filing cabinets, desk drawers, files on top of his desk, his calendar, the closet next to his desk, everywhere as quickly as I could as I knew you both would be back at any minute. Thankfully, I heard your big mouth when you two were stepping back inside and I was able to get everything back in order. Nothing really leapt out at me while we stood there and checked our paperwork, but something hit me like a ton of bricks, and I needed us to get together."

"First off, where the hell do you get off saying I have a big mouth. You don't even need cell phones around your jurisdiction, you can just shout out with that big yapper of yours. Secondly, don't keep me in suspense here. I sure as hell do not want Brice to be mixed up in this in anyway, but my ass is on the line here."

This may be stored in his closet by another employee, or it may be Brice's personal unit, I am not sure, but we need to find out. I remember you saying Lindsey spotted a correction on the packing list for a CTPAT lock and this correction was made by an electric typewriter. I did not have time to get a real close look but there was a typewriter in the closet in Brice's office. Now, maybe this is something or maybe it isn't, but I think it is worth another look. What I would like to do is get there very early in the morning and use that typewriter on a separate sheet of paper and see if we have a match. If not, we move on and try another avenue. If it is a match, we start asking questions about to whom the typewriter belongs and move forward with that person. "

"I'll be damned Sherlock. They didn't give you that badge just because your daddy was sheriff before you. You actually have some skills. Very few skills, but some skills. Let's go inside and have dinner and get some rest. I hope we have a big day tomorrow and a beginning to an end soon thereafter," Jason said.

"Look jackass. My dad was the sheriff before me, but I got the job the old-fashioned way, no one else wanted it. That little statement is also going to cost you your piece of cheesecake tonight," Ronald smiled at his friend and hugged him as they walked quickly up the driveway and inside Jason's house.

CHAPTER 7

Brice Emerges as the Villian

Ronald and Jason each stepped into the kitchen the next morning at exactly 5:00 AM. They were anxious to speak with Brice and take a look at the electric typewriter Ronald had seen in Brice's office closet. The men discussed over a hot cup of coffee how they wanted to approach the situation as Brice was an old friend of Jason's, but this clue was too crucial to the mystery that Jason knew the questions had to be asked. They finished their coffee and Lindsey walked into the kitchen as they were getting up from the table. She kissed her husband and wished him good luck today. She touched Ronald gently on the arm and with a small tear in her eye thanked him for going over and above to help Jason and the family. Ronald assured her that she and Jason would do the same for him and he was not only honored to help but it was his duty. The men climbed into Ronald's cruiser and headed for Staley's Trucking.

The morning traffic was a little heavier than what the men encountered yesterday morning, but they arrived in the parking lot of Staley's at 6:30 AM. As usual Kelly's car was already in the parking lot and the men could see the lights on in the waiting area surrounding Kelly's workstation. Jason remarked that Kelly must sleep in the parking lot or never sleep as she was always the first one there and most days one of the last to leave. She was always bright eyed and had a smile on her face. The two men walked up the steps and through the front door. Kelly greeted them and knew they were heading to Brice's office. She pointed to the office and told them she would stop by in an hour or so and see if they needed anything. Jason was growing more and more anxious as the time drew near for Brice to arrive and the difficult questions would have to be asked. Jason heard Ronald speak to Kelly and then he almost fainted dead away from what he heard after Ronald said hello to her and wished her a good morning.

"Excuse me, Kelly. May I call you Kelly or do you prefer Ms. Parton?"

"Sweetheart as good looking as you are, you can call me anything you like. I would prefer you call me for dinner sometime." Kelly had obviously taken a liking to Ronald and had turned on her Southern feminine charm. Her smile had become larger, and she was looking Ronald over from top to bottom at this point.

"I am flattered. You are a very pretty lady and the men must flock to you. I wish I could call you for dinner sometime but there is a five-foot two-inch lady in Glynn County who might strangle me if she knew I was even this close to such a lovely creature.' Ronald, too, knew how to turn on the charm but he was spoken for back home and loved his girlfriend there very much.

"Well hell. I am always a bridesmaid but never a bride," Kelly continued to smile and winked at Ronald.

Ronald propped up on Kelly's desk and bent over slightly. "Do you own or use an electric typewriter for some of your administrative work or documents?" This was the question that made Jason even weaker in the knees. Jason was thinking. "What the hell are you doing Ronald."

"For such a handsome man, you must not know much about a modern lady, sugar. I wouldn't know how to plug one of those damn things up and could probably not even spot one at first glance. You see, like my wardrobe and choice in men, my equipment must be new, fresh, and easy to use." Kelly had leaned a little closer to Ronald and had flashed a bit of her bosom at him as she answered.

Ronald was turning a shade of pink to red and knew he had been outmatched on this exchange. He smiled at Kelly and thanked her for clarifying. He slowly lifted himself off the desk and walked toward Jason who was now leaning against the wall to support his ever-weakening knees. The men walked into Brice's office and Jason fell into a chair at the mahogany desk they worked from the day before.

"What the hell was that all about, Sheriff," Jason asked once his voice returned to him from the shaking and case of nerves.

"Just working the case buddy and who knows, if things go wrong for me back home, she may be the next Mrs. Watts," Ronald joked as he could see Jason was super stressed at this point.

"Do you think she is a suspect"?

"I don't think she is, but I am not about to leave a single stone unturned my friend. This is your life we are talking about here and I need to and will question everyone. Who know, she may have mentioned who owned an electric typewriter here and can unlock our first solid clue. Besides, she wanted to check out the goods here buddy and I could not deny her that simple pleasure," Ronald was laughing hysterically now, and Jason had managed to crack a smile himself.

As the two men sat and awaited Brice, they heard Kelly greet him about ten minutes after they had made their way into his office. They heard Brice ask her to grab some coffee and bring it in when she had a minute. They could hear Brice walking swiftly down the corridor. Brice stepped inside the office and tossed his briefcase on top of his desk. He greeted the two men and shook their hands. He then went behind his desk and sat down.

"What were you guys able to ascertain yesterday or last night, guys?" Brice asked

"Brice, let me start by saying something, please. Jason was uneasy about my asking you the questions I am going to need to ask today, and he even wanted me to avoid the questions at all costs. However, as I explained to Jason that this is his life we are talking about here and I care about him as a friend. I know you feel the same way and I hope that anything I ask, and we discuss does not come off as a personal assault or any implications of any sort. I am an officer of the law and I have become numb to certain things in the pursuit of the truth. With that being said, I know Lindsey had seen some documents which had been altered by what appears to be an electric typewriter. We believe these documents and someone with access to the typewriter or who owns one here may be the first domino to fall in this investigation. I spoke with your secretary, Ms. Parton, and she assured me she does not own nor would know how to operate an electric typewriter. Do you own one Brice or have access to one?" Ronald was professional and kind in his tone but very direct and authoritative at the same time.

Brice leaned forward and cleared his throat. Just as he was about to speak, there was a soft knock on his office door and Kelly popped her head inside. She asked the men if they would like some coffee as she had it on a cart in the corridor. Brice nodded affirmably and leaned back in desk. Kelly pushed the cart inside the office and began to set three cups in line. Brice told her it was not necessary for her to pour the coffee and the men could get themselves a cup when they were ready. Kelly smiled at everyone and quietly slipped out of the office. Brice leaned forward and rested his arms on top of his desk and looked intently at Jason and then Ronald.

"I am not insulted, nor do I think you should examine every available clue and individual until you find out who set Jason up for this crime. I think of Jason more as family than an employee and I will do anything to help. I mean ANYTHING."

"So, do you own or have access to an electric typewriter," Ronald had taken a few steps closer to Brice's desk as Brice reclined in the swivel leather chair which rested behind his desk.

"I do not own one nor do I have access to one. We can look around the offices and see if someone has one in their desks. The rest of the clerical staff will be here in about twenty minutes, if you want to take a look in their offices before, they arrive for the day," Brice said. He was firm in his response and Jason and Ronald could sense a slight tone of indignation in his voice.

"Jason and I appreciate your willingness to assist in every way. I know these questions sound derogatory, but I am simply putting his best interest in front of me."

"No need to apologize and I am sorry if I seem aggravated. It is just the fact that I love Jason and would never do anything to discredit him or cause him pain. If you guys can wait up front by Kelly's desk, I will get the master key to the office doors and meet you there in a couple of minutes."

Jason and Ronald stepped outside, and Jason began to walk up the corridor towards Kelly's desk. He turned to say something to Ronald and saw him down on one knee and staring into the keyhole of Brice's office door. Jason quietly slipped back down to where Ronald was kneeling and looked at him inquisitively. Suddenly Ronald thrust the door open as Brice was closing one of his side desk drawers.

"I am all finished here and ready to go," Brice said in a startled and shaking voice.

"What do you have in the desk?" Ronald asked as Jason had now made his way into the office and was standing beside Brice. Ronald was still standing by the open office door staring sternly at the desk drawer Brice had just closed.

"There are work related files and material in there. Normal day-to-day operational things," Brice was visibly nervous, and he side stepped Jason and attempted to move towards the door.

"Please open the desk, Brice. I need to see what you placed in there," Ronald was still locked onto the desk drawer and had not looked up at Brice.

"There is some confidential material in there and I would prefer not to allow just anyone to look it over," Brice's voice was cracking more and more as he spoke.

74

"Listen, no one is leaving this office until I see what you were placing in that desk drawer. I do not want to get a warrant, but I have the Fulton County sheriff's number saved in my cell phone," Ronald was now growing angry and tired of the excuses Brice was using to avoid opening the desk drawer.

"It is not what you think Ronald," Brice was looking apologetically at Jason as he began to tear up.

"If it is not what I think then open the damn desk drawer and let me have a look at what is in there," Ronald now made his way over to the desk and was pointing at the drawer.

Brice slowly pulled the key to the drawer from his slack pocket and inserted it into the desk lock. He slowly pulled the drawer open and stared at Jason as the drawer revealed its contents. Jason lunged at Brice and shoved him up against the wall behind the desk. He had begun to slap him uncontrollably and rip away at Brice's polo shirt. Brice was now sobbing, and tears and mucus were streaming down his face from his eyes and nose.

"You son-of-a-bitch. You set me up. I thought we were friends. No! I thought we were FAMILY. You pull this shit on me. You better have some damn good answers and start talking now," Jason had released his hold on Brice's shirt and shoved him down into the swivel desk chair and stood over him fuming with rage.

Kelly suddenly appeared in the office and asked what all the commotion was about, and she had heard their voices all the way up front at her workstation. Brice, still sobbing, looked up at Kelly and told her all was well and please close the door behind her and hold all calls and visitors. She reluctantly did as she was asked, and they heard her footsteps as she made her way back to her work area.

"Start explaining NOW, Brice and I hope you have a very good explanation for this," Ronald had pulled Jason over to the mahogany table and gently pushed him into a chair as he spoke to Brice.

"You don't understand. I had no choice. The leader of the syndicate who has been running drugs, money, and human trafficking through my trucks and business threatened to kill me and my family, if I didn't set Jason up. He was asking too many damn questions about Windsor and that is the main hub of the operation. That is where the process begins. The drugs, the money, the women. It all starts in Windsor. The leader is a ruthless guy, and the syndicate does not care who they destroy or kill in the process. It is too big to be taken down. It cannot be stopped. I got in too deep. I got greedy and when I tried to back out, it was too late. I knew too much and was in too deep." Brice was still sobbing and shaking in fear and shame as he spoke.

"When Ronald told me he saw that damn typewriter, I did not want to believe it. Now you're shoving it in a desk drawer trying to hide it and keep my ass on the hook for running drugs. You are a piece of garbage man. I trusted you and you set me up. I want you to give Ronald the names of everyone here at Staley's who is involved and Windsor and wherever the hell else you scumbags do business. These are people's lives you are screwing with. Then you are going to give Ronald a full statement so he can exonerate me and arrest your ass," Jason said. He was fighting the temptation to leap out of his chair and beat Brice into confession and submission.

"I will hand over the typewriter to Ronald now and give him a sworn written statement on the drugs being planted in your container the day you were caught in Brunswick. I need to please get my affairs in order and then I will meet you all at the Sheriff's Office here in Atlanta and provide a detailed list of names, distribution locations, EVERYTHING. I just need twenty-four hours to get my affairs lined up and my family to safety. Please, please give me the twenty-four hours. They will kill my family, if I don't get them to a safe haven." Brice was sobbing more uncontrollably now than ever before.

"You will get your twenty-four hours. I will have a deputy with the Fulton County Sheriff's Office shadow you and provide protection for you until we arrive at your home tomorrow morning. First things first, why don't you get that typewriter you're so fond of and type a letter clearing Jason and sign it right now," Ronald slammed the typewriter down on top of Brice's desk and pointed furiously at it.

As Brice began to type out the letter stating he was responsible for placing the drugs in Jason's container, modifying his documents, and making the anonymous call to the Glynn County Sheriff's Office that fateful day, Ronald was on the phone with Keith Powers, the Fulton County Sheriff, briefing him on the events of the morning and the information Brice had provided and would provide. Ronald explained how they would need a deputy for the next twenty-four hours to protect and keep Brice from fleeing the area. Sheriff Powers agreed to assist in any way that his office could and let Ronald know a deputy would be at Staley's Trucking within the hour. As Ronald was finishing his call with Powers, Brice was removing the paper from the carriage of the typewriter and signing and dating the document. He handed it over to Ronald and Ronald folded the document and placed it in his front shirt pocket. Brice looked over at Jason with tears still streaming down his cheeks and tried to offer an apology.

"Kiss my ass and I hope you rot in prison for what you did to me and those poor women. You are pathetic and I hope the damn money was worth it. Maybe you can buy some sympathy from someone but it sure as hell will not be me," Jason shoved Brice out of his way and stormed down the corridor to exit the building.

As Jason was walking by her desk, Kelly asked him if everything was alright. Jason stopped and looked at her and said, "not by a long shot." Kelly quickly expressed concern, but Jason had already shoved the front door open and allowed it to slam behind him as he walked down the steps and into the parking lot.

The Fulton County deputy arrived and escorted Brice to his cruiser and allowed him to sit in the front seat. The deputy walked over and introduced himself to Ronald as Deputy Wallace Wilkes. Deputy Wilkes gave Ronald his personal cell number and assured him Brice would be under surveillance until he arrived the next day. Ronald thanked him and walked over to his own cruiser where Jason had already climbed into the front seat and was waiting for him to arrive and drive him home. Ronald explained he would take him home and head immediately for Brunswick. He would get this signed confession to the judge in Jason's case and have the district attorney dismiss the charges against him and file the necessary paperwork before the close of business today. Ronald attempted to console his friend, but Jason sat there and murmured obscenities under his breath about Brice and the entire situation. The ride to Jason's home was more of the same. Jason climbed out of the cruiser when it pulled into his driveway, he walked around to the driver's side and motioned for Ronald to roll down the window. Ronald rolled down the window and his friend leaned into the car and hugged his friend. He thanked him and turned to walk to his front door. Ronald told him he would call once all the paperwork was filed with the courts and would stay at his own home tonight. He assured Jason that he would be back at Jason's home tomorrow morning by 6:00 AM and they would drive to Brice's together. He made Jason promise that he would stay home and not try to contact Brice. Jason begrudgingly promised his friend and told him he would see him in the morning. Jason waved to Ronald as he drove away and walked through the door of his home. He would have great news for Lindsey about his situation but not so good news about Brice and his betrayal.

CHAPTER 8

The Answers Stop and
More Questions Arise

The following morning Jason was sitting in his and Lindsey's lawn swing drinking his morning coffee and awaiting sunrise and his friend Ronald. Jason had experienced a sleepless night as he replayed over and over in his mind how Brice could have become involved in such a despicable situation, how long had it been going on, how many women were involved in the human trafficking, who was the kingpin, and who were the major players in this criminal enterprise. As the sun was just creeping up over the horizon, he saw car headlights turning into his driveway. He didn't need to check the time as he knew Ronald was always a little early and always on time. Ronald turned off the engine and walked up and took a seat by his friend.

"Now don't confuse me for Lindsey and try to steal an early morning kiss. I know I'm sexy, but I like to get my kisses from someone with a little less facial hair than yours," Ronald said with a small laugh as he patted his friend on the leg as reassurance all was well.

"You would be lucky to get a kiss from a handsome dude like me. You would never be the same. On a serious note, thanks for calling me last night and confirming my innocence with the court and handling it so quickly. My next concern is getting all this information from Brice and making sure these drugs and human trafficking gets stopped immediately. All I could think about last night was that it could be Lindsey or my girls someday and it makes me sick to my stomach," Jason hugged his friend again, stood up, and made his way to the passenger seat of Ronald's cruiser.

Brice lived on a large farm outside the city limits north of Atlanta and they had at least an hour and a half drive ahead of them with the morning traffic. The two friends talked about the situation and hoped that Brice had all the information needed to shut this gruesome syndicate down. Ronald explained to Jason he was to be there only as an observer and a material witness but was to leave questioning and legal wrangling to himself and the Fulton County Sheriff's Office. Jason was not overly thrilled about those arrangements but agreed to abide by them as he wanted to help in any capacity that he could. They pulled up at Brice's property at 7:45 AM. They found Sheriff Powers standing beside his cruiser facing a large, red painted barn about forty yards away from his cruiser. When Ronald and Jason walked up, Powers explained that Brice had walked his family out to the barn to get his wife and three children into a minivan and send them safely through the rear of the property to avoid the main roadways. Brice signaled to Powers once the minivan was loaded and pulled away, disappearing into the darkness of the rear of his property. Brice had called out to Powers letting him know he was packing up a few items to take with him to the courthouse and would be at his cruiser in five minutes.

"How long ago was it that he called out to you, Powers?" Ronald asked.

"It was about four minutes or so before you guys pulled up."

"He has had long enough. Whatever he doesn't have by now, he can send for later, or make it alright without it. He needs to get his ass out here now." Ronald was somewhat frustrated that Powers had allowed Brice that much latitude. Powers explained he was securing the perimeter and not allowing him access to automobiles behind him. Ronald was not impressed, but felt it was not the time to address the issue.

Ronald called out to Brice and demanded he come out from the barn immediately. The three men began to walk towards the barn and Ronald's calls became louder and more forceful. By the time they reached the barn door, Ronald was shouting at the top of his lungs and had begun to use obscenities in his orders for Brice.

As they rounded the corner, Ronald was in the lead with Powers trailing closely behind and Jason about five yards behind them. Suddenly Ronald pulled his weapon from the holster and threw up his free hand for Powers to circle over to the opposite side of the entrance across from them. Once Powers was in motion, Ronald used the same free hand and motioned for Jason to stand firm where he was located.

"Damn it." Ronald blurted out as he stared menacingly at Powers.

Jason came running up and stopped beside Ronald. He glanced over at Powers who was frozen in space and had a look of disappointment and bewilderment on his face. Jason looked over at Ronald who had now turned around and viciously kicked the barn door and glared back at Powers. Jason inadvertently looked inside the barn while waiting for Ronald to speak and saw what the frustration stemmed from. There swinging from the flooring of the second story hay storage area dangling some twenty feet from the first level of the barn was Brice Staley. A noose was around his neck, and he was no longer breathing. At this point, Ronald shouted out to Powers to call for additional support, an ambulance, and the coroner. Jason moved toward the ladder to climb up into the second-floor hay storage area. His intention was to cut his old friend and boss down to preserve some dignity for him before the additional support arrived. Ronald shouted at Jason to stop before he had placed his leg on the second rung of the old wooden ladder. Jason did not want to comply but did not want to comprise Ronald's authority or investigation, either.

The three men stood in silence each man looking over at Brice's lifeless body swinging from the second story floor, down to the ground, and then at each other. Powers was visibly shaken, and, in his heart, he knew Ronald would not have a favorable report to share with his superiors with the Sheriff's Association. Ronald could only keep thinking to himself what a rookie mistake Powers had made and how the only damn witness they had was now dead via suicide or murder. Jason's thoughts turned from sympathy for the death of his former friend and then his thoughts echoed Ronald's that their one solid lead was now dead.

It seemed like hours but only about twenty-five minutes, the sirens of five additional Sheriff's cars, an ambulance, and the coroner's van arrived. Deputies hurriedly filed out of their cruisers, two paramedics came swiftly up to the entrance of the barn pushing a gurney, and the coroner slowly brought up the rear of the caravan. One of the deputies climbed up the ladder Jason tried to ascend earlier and made his way over to the spot where the rope had been attached to the flooring. He gently pulled up on the rope and brought Brice's corpse up to the top level of the barn. He called down to confirm what everyone in attendance knew, that Brice Staley was deceased. The coroner gave the order for the body to be brought down to ground level so she could begin her investigation and secure the body for a proper autopsy at the crime lab. The paramedics stood by in case they were called upon but were soon released by Sheriff Powers and the coroner. Ronald walked over to the body to have a glance for any type of clue. He had every intention of following the coroner to the crime lab. An initial glance showed nothing out of the ordinary, but he still wanted to be there for the autopsy. The process took over three hours to canvas the area, secure the body, and release everyone in attendance. Sheriff Powers held two of his deputies and posted one at each entrance of the barn. He instructed them to ensure no one entered the area and the scene was to remain intact until he and Sheriff Watts returned for their own examination. He told them he would send someone to relieve them later this afternoon but make certain the integrity of the scene was not disturbed and they were not to leave for any reason until relieved. Jason and Ronald were making their way to Ronald's cruiser when Sheriff Powers called out to Ronald.

"Sheriff Watts. I know you think I made the largest rookie mistake on the planet back there. In all honesty, you could not be more correct. I have been an officer of the law for thirteen years and sheriff for another seven. I want you to know, I am sending in a report of this incident and my mistake to the Sheriff's Association, and I am sure they will forward it to the governor. There is no excuse but let me share my thought process at the time with you, please. Brice had just seen his family up at the house and he told them he was not sure how this was going to work out or how long they would need to be gone. He admitted to framing Jason Jennings and knew he had to pay for that mistake. He asked me if he could accompany them and have just a few minutes of time with them for what may be a very, very long time. I am a dad and husband. I let my personal feelings get in the way of correct legal protocol and know it may impact the case long term. I made a massive mistake, and I am sorry," Powers was professional and sincere in his tone.

"Well sheriff. If you did not get one thing right today, you sure as hell got the massive mistake right. I appreciate your taking ownership of this error in judgement and handling this up the chain of command. It makes things easier because I was without a shadow of a doubt going to ensure this saw the desk of the association with a recommendation to forward to the governor. I cannot imagine how a man with over twenty years of service could handle a situation with such neolithic incompetence. If this corpse proves to be a dead end and we find no more clues, it will not be the last time you are sorry. Your ass can bank on that, Sheriff Powers. I need to go and I hope our paths do not cross anymore on this investigation," Ronald was red-faced and slowly backing away from Powers as he feared he may grab Powers or punch him in the mouth.

"Let's go Jason. Time to clean up someone's damn spilled milk. What a damn joke."

Jason climbed into the passenger seat of the cruiser and dared not say anything immediately. He rode in silence for the next fifteen miles and finally summoned the courage to speak. "Look. I know you are pissed, and I am not a law enforcement officer by any stretch of the imagination. The guy screwed up and screwed up HUGE. He deserved to take a hit but weren't you a little tough on the guy?"

"Hell no. He knows better and I promise if there are not any clues on the corpse or found at the crime scene, this bozo has not seen or heard the last of me. What a damn IDIOT! Jason, we need to talk about the legalities of your arrangement now. I don't believe Powers would make an issue about your being an observer on this case, but it was based on you being a material witness. This is still valid, but I would rather make it ironclad to avoid any potential retaliation from Powers, if he became angry enough. Please raise your right hand and I am going to swear you in as a temporary deputy of the county of Glynn." Ronald swore Jason in as a temporary deputy and did manage to make a small quip about him not being allowed to carry a weapon and asked him not to get silly and attempt to arrest someone. He asked Jason to retrieve a badge from the glove compartment as Ronald kept one there for temporary deputies, in case of emergencies. They each chuckled a bit but the seriousness of the matter regained control of the drive.

Jason let the balance of the drive to the crime lab be in silence as he knew Ronald was not going to be talked into a differing opinion or be calmed at this juncture. The ride was another fifteen miles. They arrived in front of the crime lab and made their way into the building. The front desk acknowledged that they were expected and showed them to the examination room in which Brice had been wheeled. They entered the room and saw the forensic coroner examining the body.

"Good afternoon gentlemen. My name is Dr. Edna. I am the chief medical examiner for Fulton County. I understand this man may have been a material witness or perhaps even a suspect in a joint investigation with the FBI, Glynn County, and Fulton County," Dr. Edna snapped off her blue surgical gloves off after she covered the body with a sheet and then extended her hand towards Ronald.

"Yes, he is or was." Ronald spoke up as he shook Dr. Edna's hand.

"I wanted to discuss a few things with you in private," Dr. Edna looked over at Jason and then at her assistant. The assistant briskly walked to the door of the examination room and disappeared down the corridor. Dr. Edna, expecting Jason to follow the assistant out of the room, stood stone-like staring at him.

"I have duly deputized this man. I would like to introduce myself and him. I am Sheriff Ronald Watts of Glynn County, and this is my temporary deputy, Jason Jennings."

"My apologies to you and your deputy. You could see how it may be a bit confusing as he is not dressed in an officer's uniform nor displaying his badge. No problem here. Let me discuss what my preliminary examination has unearthed and show you the personal effects Mr. Staley had on his person when he arrived at our facility," Dr. Edna moved back over to the examination table on which Brice was lying and pulled the sheet back exposing his naked, stiffening body.

Dr. Edna began to show both men how the cause of death was strangulation brought on by the hangman's noose. She explained that at first observation it appeared to be a suicide. She explained she ruled out the suicide theory after examining the bruises on the knuckles of Brice's right hand. He had apparently struck his assailant causing bruising to his hand. After Dr. Edna saw the bruises, she continued a more thorough examination of the body and found where Brice had been injected with Thiopental. She explained Thiopental had not been available in the United States since 2010. This means whoever committed this murder has underground connections and knows some dangerous and lethal people. There were no skin traces from the killer and no fingerprints found on the clothing. The killer had to have used gloves to inject the Thiopental and conduct the hanging. Dr. Edna explained she had found something in the bottom of Brice's left shoe. There were no belongings found on his person, but this note was placed in a small envelope and between his sock and shoe. She explained that whoever had committed the murder had removed all his belongings in an attempt to ensure he was not leaving any traces of suspicion or clues for whomever found the body. The killer had to move swiftly as they knew Sheriff Powers was outside the barn and would come inside if Brice was not outside when he requested. Dr. Edna handed the envelope and containing the note to Ronald. Ronald was already on his cell phone calling Sheriff Powers to ensure the area at Brice's home and especially his barn was locked down. As soon as Sheriff Powers confirmed the areas were secure, Ronald hung up and opened the envelope.

CHAPTER 9

Has the Kingpin Been Identified?

Ronald slowly opened the envelope and began to unwrap the tightly folded note which was housed inside. He looked up and stared at Jason. He shook his head from side-to-side and looked intently at the unwrapped piece of paper. Jason inched closer to Ronald and began to look at the note, also.

"What the hell does this mean, Ronald?

"I am not sure. What does 'the qb holds the key' mean. What is Brice trying to reveal? He was a huge football fan and followed the Georgia Bulldogs religiously every year. Who is their QB or quarterback? Is there some link to the quarterback for the Dawgs or another team to what the hell is going with his company? Did he know any of the players? Maybe he was going to leave us some form of a clue at his office at home or his office at Staley's Trucking. What we need to do now Jason is split up and each one of us takes an office. You get an UBER, and head out to Staley's Trucking and check his office there. I will ride out to Brice's farm and canvas hos office and the barn area where the murder took place. Call me as soon as you check everything in that office and Staley's and then get an UBER out to the farm. I am sure checking his home, and the murder scene will take longer than your check at Staley's.

The two men split up after thanking Dr. Edna for all her support and information. Ronald left a business card with her and asked that she call him with any updates she may have surrounding Brice's examination. Jason's UBER arrived at Staley's trucking forty-five minutes later and he texted Ronald letting him know he had arrived there. Ronald text back about fifteen minutes later letting him know he was at Brice's farm along with Sheriff Powers and three other deputies who had secured the area to ensure everything was intact at the time of the murder.

Jason raced up the steps to the main office entrance of Staley's Trucking and saw Kelly sitting quietly at her desk. She had obviously been crying and was very emotional. She had gotten word about Brice from the television news in Atlanta and had not been able to focus since the heartbreaking announcement. Jason circled behind her desk and hugged her and told her not to worry that Brice's killer would be brought to justice. She nodded in the affirmative and managed to thank Jason for his concern and she wanted to help anyway she could. Jason explained that he had to check out some files in Brice's office and he should not be long. Kelly just nodded yes and buried her head in her hands again and began to cry uncontrollably.

Jason entered Brice's office and pulled the door shut behind him. He searched every file and every scrap of paperwork he could in the office to no avail. His desk calendar had no special notes and no special meeting scheduled. Just the normal day-to-day business operations for Staley's Trucking. He noticed his laptop was missing and he text Ronald to check for it at Brice's home. Jason knew the IT team with the Fulton County Sheriff's Office or the GBI could bypass the login requirements and check the contents of the laptop. About ten minutes later, Ronald texted back and stated he had found the laptop on Brice's desk in his office at home. Jason did a second sweep of everything he had checked previously and still nothing related to the 'qb' reference. He decided to grab an UBER and head to Brice's farm. As he walked down the corridor and back by Kelly's desk, he saw her still sitting stoically in silence and wiping tears from her cheeks. Jason stopped to hug her once more and ask her to head home for the day. He would work with Brice's minority ownership group to see how they wanted to proceed from a business standpoint tomorrow morning. For the time being, Jason recommended that no more loading or transaction take place until the group could reach a decision on plans forward. He knew it was late in the afternoon and most of the drivers were either at home, down for their required DOT shutdown rest hours, or at their delivery locations. He asked Kelly if anyone had checked in as he knew it would not be long before everyone knew of the murder and would be asking about a path forward for the organization. He asked Kelly if she felt up to it to send a group text to all the drivers and let them know the situation and a decision would be reached soon on resuming scheduling. Kelly agreed and would leave for the day after sending the message and locking the office.

"Kelly, one other quick question. Who is still running today? I know you can track the drivers' locations and movements with the software downloaded on their rigs. I just want to ensure these drivers wrap up and head home until the minority ownership gives us clear direction."

"The only three drivers still out running are Bobby Kraft, Quinn Brown, and Derrick Downs. As luck would have it, they are all three making deliveries in the metro area today. I know Quinn is finished for the day because he called me mid-morning and told me his software had crashed on his rig and he did not want me or the dispatchers to think he was not running today. Thanks for caring Jason and I appreciate your concern for me and everyone here at Staley's. You are a good man."

As Jason was opening the office door, he saw his UBER arriving in the parking lot. He climbed in the back seat and the UBER raced away towards Brice's farm. Jason continued to turn the note over and over in his head and he was still in disbelief that Brice was dead. The UBER ride took a little over an hour as the afternoon traffic had begun in the metro area. When it arrived at Brice's farm Jason thanked the driver and made his way toward the barn where he saw Ronald standing in the doorway assessing the area. Ronald had been inside the home, and more importantly, Brice's office since he had arrived a couple of hours ago. He turned to see the UBER pulling up and Jason exiting the car. He smiled at Jason and waved for him to come over to the barn entrance. Jason was moving hastily that way when suddenly, he stopped dead in his tracks. He stood there staring into space and you could almost see the wheels turning inside his head. Ronald called out for him to come over but Jason stood firmly and stared more and more intently into space.

Ronald walked hurriedly over to where Jason was standing and stopped about two feet from his friend. "What the hell is up with you man? Do you need to take the afternoon off? I know you and Brice were close and this cannot be easy for you. "

Jason stood still and did not acknowledge Ronald's presence. Finally, like he was snapping out of a trance looked blankly at Ronald. "No, no, no man I'm good, "Jason stammered mildly.

"Did you see a ghost, Jason? Do you need something to drink? Maybe you should sit down for a few minutes."

"Let's talk buddy," Jason blurted out as if Ronald had not been speaking to him.

Jason grabbed Ronald by the arm and escorted him over to Ronald's cruiser. He asked Ronald for the note found on Brice's body. Ronald produced the note and handed it to Jason. The two men leaned up against the hood of the cruiser and Jason stared at the note. Several minutes passed and Ronald did not say anything as he wanted to allow Jason to process his thoughts and allow him the opportunity to speak first. Ronald could not stand the silence any longer and turned and faced Jason.

"Ok man. What the hell is up? What are you thinking?"

"When I was leaving the office this afternoon, I stopped to check on Kelly and asked her to message the drivers to let them know we would be suspending operations until I could speak to the minority partners and see how they wanted to move forward. She told me there were only three drivers still delivering and the others were on DOT required rest or home. She said one of the driver's software was broken and had checked in with her this morning to let her and the dispatchers know he was running but could not be tracked. I did not think anything about it until I saw you standing in front of the barn, and it hit like a ton of bricks. This may not be anything but it sure as hell seems like too much of a coincidence. The driver whose software was down and working the metro area today was Quinn. The driver was Quinn Brown," Jason stood there now staring sharply at Ronald.

"I'll be damned. Quinn Brown, qb. What could be his motive? Damn, damn, damn," Ronald was now processing information a mile a minute and staring into space much like Jason was earlier.

"Let's take a ride out to Quinn's house. He lives about twenty-five minutes from Brice's farm and that's with regular metro-area traffic. He could make it quicker if the traffic cooperated. If he is the guy we are looking for, I want to know why he could ever get involved in something like this."

Ronald turned on the siren and his flashing lights to ensure traffic moved out of their path as he wanted to speak with Quinn immediately. They may be close to getting answers and shutting down this trafficking and drug running operation. Ronald knew what he was doing was out of his jurisdiction for high-speed action, but he did not care at this point. They arrived at Quinn's house in less than twenty minutes and saw his rig parked alongside the right side of his home and property. Jason verified that his wife's car and Quinn's car were both in the driveway. Quinn should be home. They parked partially behind both vehicles where it would make it difficult to escape, if Quinn thought it might become necessary. Jason and Ronald jumped out of their seats and slammed their doors closed. They almost ran up the steps and banged on the front door as Ronald persistently rang the doorbell. This went on for nearly a full minute and they could not hear anyone moving about inside nor did anyone call out to them from inside the home. Ronald called Sheriff Powers and asked him to bring a warrant to Quinn's home so they could legally enter and search for clues and see if Quinn was hiding inside and had no intention of facing them.

Sheriff Powers came racing up the street leading to Quinn's home thirty minutes after he received the call from Ronald. He acknowledged that he had a warrant and for them to kick the door in if no one answered the next ring of the doorbell. Ronald was forced to kick the door open. The door flew open with a swiftness and dangled on one hinge as Ronald had kicked it with such veracity. The three men raced inside and each darted in a different direction throughout the home looking for Quinn Brown. They had searched the downstairs and upstairs areas and the backyard and there was no one at the residence. Sheriff Powers called into his office and instructed that there be an APB placed for Quinn Brown and his wife. The three men stepped back outside to their cruisers and stared blankly at each other for what felt like an eternity before Ronald finally spoke.

"Guys, I think I want to speak with Special Agents Wright and Wilkes. They are running the investigation into the abduction and potential trafficking of the four French girls in Laredo. I want to see if it would be possible for us to speak with those ladies and see if they might have heard something about Quinn or maybe even seen him at some point. If he is the kingpin and it looks very favorably to me that he is, maybe they overheard his name, saw his face, or be able to link him to this operation."

Powers and Jason agreed it would be the next logical step in the process until Quinn was located and brought in for questioning. Also, if they had a positive identification by one or all the French girls, then he would be more inclined to talk and divulge all the information on his operation. Ronald called Agent Wilkes on her cell number she had listed on the business card she gave to Jason when they met. Wilkes told Ronald the French girls had returned home to their families in Quebec and they were told that they may be needed for additional questioning should the need arise. Wilkes did not want the girls transported back to the US as they needed to be home with family and try to overcome the awful circumstances they were forced into. Ronald did receive permission to travel to Quebec and speak with them and Wilkes provided their contact numbers. Ronald asked Sheriff Powers to contact him the instant Quinn or his wife was located, but he and Jason would be on the first flight to Quebec tomorrow morning. They would need to return to Jason's home and pack a bag. Ronald also needed to check in with his office in Brunswick and he knew Jason wanted to see Lindsey and the girls.

The next morning Jason and Ronald headed to the Hartsfield-Jackson Airport in Atlanta for a direct flight to Quebec. The men passed through the security checkpoint, collected their suitcases, and headed for Gate 12 in Hangar F. Their flight departed on time and the flight should be just shy of five hours. Their flight should touch down in Quebec at 2:00 PM local time. The flight was a smooth one and the men took a taxi to a local hotel. They decided to call each of the girls and their families and see if they could speak with them tomorrow morning. The families agreed to meet with them, starting with the first family at 8:00 AM. Ronald and Jason grabbed a bite to eat at the hotel bistro and decided to get to bed early as tomorrow could possibly be a huge day for the investigation.

The men arose early and ate breakfast at the same bistro they had dinner at the night before. They took a cab to the first girl's home on their list, a fifteen year old named Lousie Dupont. A very petite lady answered the door at a very modest home in a neighborhood just outside the city limits of Quebec. She introduced herself as Anna Dupont and asked Ronald and Jason please step inside and sit down. Her English was somewhat broken, but she appeared to understand the spoken word very well. Jason and Ronald sat down on the sofa across from Anna's rocking chair and saw, to their surprise, five other people coming out of the back three bedrooms at the end of the home's hallway. Ronald and Jason stood up to greet them. There were four young girls and a tall, burly, balding man trailing closely behind the four girls. Ronald and Jason looked at each other, smiled at the group, and extended handshakes to each of the young girls and gentleman.

"I know this must seem as a surprise to you two gentlemen," Anna began slowly as she sat down in her rocking chair. The man had spoken something in French to the four young ladies and they disappeared briefly into the kitchen area and came back with four dining room chairs. They positioned the chairs between the rocking chair in which Anna was sitting and an old, tattered leather easy chair in which the man had taken a seat. Ronald and Jason slowly sat back down on the sofa which was ten feet or so away from the line of people in front of them.

"I want to explain," the gentlemen began and spoke in perfect English. "My name is Pierre Dupont. This is my daughter, Lousie. The other girls are our adopted daughters. They were friends of Lousie and now they are her sisters. I would like to introduce Charlotte Blanchet, Celine Dubois, and Camille Moreau. Anna and I adopted these young ladies nearly a year ago. Their parents were captured by this American you have come to Quebec to learn more about. This American is ruthless. He sold their mothers into his despicable sex trafficking ring and shot their fathers when they attempted to escape the organization the syndicate had imprisoned them in as drug runners. This is a most cruel and soulless group of individuals, and their leader is a heartless individual who has zero compassion for anyone and will eliminate anyone who stands in their way. We only gave you Lousie's address as ours as we had our friends in the Royal Canadian Mounted Police running checks on each of you before we disclosed that all the girls are our daughters now. They phoned me late last night and verified that you are who you say you are and are here to capture the head of this syndicate.

I am a retired investigator for the RCMP and still have deep connections there. We have provided them with the information we have and what our daughters could recollect. They are ardently working the case inside the Canadian border, and we hope you can work equally hard on the United States' boundaries. My daughters have suffered enough. They need a deep level of closure and the only way for this to happen is for this group to be caught, prosecuted, and shut down. Anna and I will retire to the kitchen and allow you to speak with our four girls. They know more than we but if you need to speak with us at any time, please call out and we will assist."

Pierre stood up quickly and Anna stood up almost simultaneously. Pierre spoke something in French to the girls and they nodded affirmatively. Anna and Pierre disappeared into the kitchen and gently closed the door. The four girls stared at Ronald and Jason as they joined hands. One of the girls cleared her throat and quietly spoke as Ronald and Jason inched out onto the edge of the sofa.

"My name is Celine. I am the oldest of my sisters. I am sixteen years old. Papa was right about these people, they are cruel. When they abducted us, they should us the video made of our natural parents being murdered. They told us if we did not do as we were told we would meet the same fate. I thank God for Papa Pierre and Mother Anna. They have taken us all in and treated us as one of their very own children.

"Is there anything you can tell us about the people who abducted you? Did you hear their names, nicknames, were they all men or were there some women in the group? Anything you can remember will be helpful. I know this is painful and brings up horrible memories but anything you recall will help us capture these people and ensure they are punished," Ronald inched closer to Celine as her English was very broken and sometimes difficult to understand.

They were all men. They spoke very quickly, and our English is not so good. We could not understand a lot of what they were saying. They talked about a manager at the Windsor warehouse and the manager in Georgia. I am not sure what they were talking about for certain. We saw five men that day. When we were forced to get into the trailer, we heard one of them say for the driver to be sure we did not escape when the lock was changed in Georgia. One of the English speakers shouted a word in French we did not understand. One of the men was French or knew how to speak French as he laughed at what the man said and called him an idiot.

"What did he shout?" Jason asked.

"I am not sure. It sounded like 'bonjour a la folle or maybe le fou'. The other man corrected him after he called him an idiot, but the doors were slamming, and we could not her the word or words he used to correct him. "

"What does la folle or le fou mean," Ronald was scribbling furiously as he was taking notes along with recording the conversation on his cell phone?

"La folle is what you would call an angry lady and le fou an angry man," Celine was looking disappointed as she was unable to be more precise.

"Don't be frustrated Celine. You have been a huge help. I appreciate your reliving this as I know it must be horrifying for you all," Ronald said as he was winding down the conversation. He saw it was beginning to conjure up terrible memories for all the girls.

Jason stepped into the kitchen and asked Pierre and Anna to rejoin them in the living room area. Ronald hugged all the young girls and thanked them for their courage. He had given each of them a business card with his cell number on it in case they recalled anything further. He and Jason thanked Mr. and Mrs. Dupont for their support and time and asked that they give them a call to say if the RCMP procured any leads or if the girls may recall anything.

As they were standing on the corner awaiting their taxi, Ronald suggested they return to their hotel, pack, and head to the airport to fly out to Windsor and speak with the manager of the facility there. When they arrived in Windsor, Ronald would call and see if Pierre could arrange for a member of the RCMP to accompany them to have local police presence there, if an arrest could be made. The taxi arrived and the men packed and called another taxi to take them from the hotel to the airport. They booked a flight leaving for Windsor in three hours and the flight would take almost five hours to arrive there. They grabbed a hamburger in the airport lounge and went to their gate location to sit and await the opportunity to board. The flight arrived and landed in Windsor at 6:00 PM. The men decided to get a rental car as they may need to move quickly and travel to more than one spot while in Windsor. They arrived at a local hotel around 7:00 PM, checked in and decided to turn in early and get started early the next morning. Each man was curious to hear what the manager at the Windsor warehouse would have to say. Did what he was to say that day mean anything or was it just a trivial statement made within the conversation?

The two men met the next morning at 6:00 AM in the hotel cafeteria. They ate breakfast almost in silence as the thoughts continued to race through their minds. Each man had a lot to say to Mr. Davis when they arrived at his facility and they hoped that his answers would incriminate him and his co-conspirators. They finished their breakfast and were on the freeway at 6:45 AM. They arrived at the Windsor warehouse forty-five minutes later. They parked in the visitor parking area and awaited the arrival of Inspector Nario Babin of the RCMP. He was an old friend of Pierre Dupont and agreed to assist as long as he was needed. Inspector Babin arrived fifteen minutes later, and the three men made their way towards the office area to speak with Mr. Davis.

Before they could climb the steps up into the office area, a man Jason recognized as Mr. Davis fired the glass entrance door open and stood within the doorway entrance. It seemed he was reluctant to allow the men to enter. Finally, Mr. Babin spoke and explained that they had the necessary warrant to enter the premises and Davis could speak to them willingly or they could ask him to accompany them down to his office for a more formal discussion as his officers would be here searching all offices, computers, and questioning every employee at the facility. Rowland reluctantly stepped aside and told them his office was the last office down the corridor on the left. The four men entered the office and took seats around an oak meeting table centered in the spacious office area.

"We need answers. Straight answers and information, Mr. Davis. We will not tolerate stonewalling and half-truths. My office is prepared to shut down this operation and do an intensive search of all records and personnel, if we feel that we do not have your full cooperation." Inspector Babin was forceful in his tone and looked intently at Mr. Davis as he spoke.

"I am fully prepared to answer any and all questions any of you may have. I want to admit that I was privy to unlawful acts here at the facility but I, in no way, orchestrated the actions or participated any more than allowing the kingpin to utilize my warehouse location for distribution of narcotics."

"Is narcotics all you were allowing the kingpin and their syndicate to pass through your operation," Ronald had inched closer toward the table and was now sitting literally on the edge of his chair?

"No sir. I know where you are heading with your next question, and I became aware of the human trafficking going on. It sickens me but I was in too deep. The kingpin is brutal and human life means nothing to them. I was assured that the money, which I no longer wanted, would only increase but if I talked, they knew my family's daily routine, where I lived, and promised to systematically kill them off one by one and kill me last so I could suffer having to bury my three children and wife. None of this makes what I did forgivable or excusable. I simply need my family to be protected. I am willing to testify to everything I know and provide any information you need. I do not give a damn about what happens to me anymore. I do still love my family and want them to be relocated and safe."

"The families of those young girls and poison you allowed to be shipped to ruin lives certainly give a damn. You sit here and think we should have pity on your sorry ass and give a damn about those crocodile tears you are shedding. KISS MY ASS! I hope they bury your ass in prison and then let God take his vengeance." Jason who had been primarily a silent observer, had become massively angered at Rowland's confession.

Ronald reached out for his friend and gently pushed him back against the chair he had begun to rise from as he stared angrily at Mr. Davis. "Listen the only way you get cooperation from the United States, and I am sure the Canadian government will feel the same way, is to give us names, contacts, delivery locations, the entire operation and that begins with the kingpin's name and how you make contact."

Mr. Davis inched back into his chair and buried his face in his hands. He was sobbing uncontrollably and kept muttering under his breath about how in the hell he let himself get involved in such a despicable operation. He looked up at the three men staring at him with icy cold looks of determination, disgust, and anger. He wiped his eyes with a handkerchief he drew from his back pocket and gently cleared his throat.

"Please remember to help my family," Davis pleaded with the men as he began to sob again.

"Listen here you son-of-a-bitch. If you don't start talking right now, I am going to have the Inspector and Ronald look the other way while I beat the living hell out of you and then give them a turn. You start talking now and if the next words out of your mouth is not the person behind this depraved operation, I promise to kick your ass from here to Pierre Dupont's home and I assure you he will not give a damn about your apologies and how terribly you feel," Jason had now sprung from his seat and grabbed Rowland by his shirt collar on either sides and was slamming him back and forth against the chair's backing.

Nario and Ronald grabbed Jason by each of his arms and dragged him across the room. Ronald gently pinned him against the wall and was quietly asking him to calm down. The men knew if Jason continued the chances of him killing Mr. Davis was high. Ronald spun around still holding Jason firmly but not as to hurt him and told Davis he had about four seconds to give them the name or he was about to let Jason free, and Jason could make good on his promise.

"The name of the kingpin, who is known as qb, is Quinn Brown. He is the man who is the head of this syndicate and oversees all orders given and deadly enforcement of those not followed. Now please dispatch someone to protect my family and get them relocated."

Jason and Ronald stood frozen staring at each other. They each wanted to speak but were too shocked to speak. Inspector Babin was calling his office to have Mr. Davis's family located, guarded, and prepared to be in protective custody until a trial could be arranged and Rowland was to testify. He then placed Rowland under arrest and handcuffed him. Ronald asked Nario to please contact them with any and every update and that he and Jason would probably be heading back to the US to assist with the location efforts of Quinn Brown. They were going to call Sheriff Powers in Atlanta and Special Agents Wright and Wilkes to let them know about Rowland's confession and his implication of Quinn Brown as the kingpin of the syndicate. They wanted efforts doubled in an attempt to locate Quinn and begin to bring the kidnapped girls home that he had enabled to be trafficked.

CHAPTER 10

Back to Atlanta and the Hunt for Quinn Brown

Jason and Ronald arranged for flights back to Atlanta after contacting Powers. Wilkes, and Wright. Their first order of business would be to meet with the three of them and see where they could best be utilized in the search for Quinn. Jason recommended stopping by and speaking with Kelly at Staley's Trucking and seeing if she might have heard from him at some off chance or if someone had contacted her about his salary payment. Special Agents Wilkes and Wright had Kelly suspend his direct deposit and they had frozen his accounts. Jason knew Kelly could write him a regular payroll check if direct deposit was not available. Quinn would need money, if his cash was depleted and accounts locked. Quinn could use any of his syndicates contacts to get cash, but the men were just hoping for any slip up on Quinn's part at this juncture.

The flight into Atlanta landed at 4:00 AM the next morning. Jason and Ronald had showered at the airport in Canada as they awaited their flight to board. The two men decided they would head directly to Staley's after running through a fast-food drive through and get a breakfast sandwich and some coffee. Jason had text Kelly earlier in the week and asked if the minority partners were still providing service to the customers. She confirmed that they were, but custom agents were at every pick-up and delivery location to ensure nothing was being illegally transported by Staley's employees. This would be a common practice moving forward until a new ownership base was in place and the government was 100% convinced no further illegal activity was ongoing. The men arrived at Staley's around 6:00 AM and saw Kelly's car already in the parking lot.

"Good morning, young lady. How are you today? I see you still get here early and stay late. How's business been?" Jason greeted Kelly as they walked up to her desk area.

Kelly beamed a beautiful, bright smile as she pushed her long hair back behind her ears. "Life is good. I just wish the investigation would come to a close and solve these issues surrounding Staley's. The minority partners have secured two very interested organizations who would both like to buy the business and continue to operate out of Atlanta but they both are reluctant to become fully committal until the investigation wraps and the government has ended its involvement in the day-to-day operations. Do you know if there are any new leads?"

"Well, to be honest." Jason began to respond when Ronald stepped up beside him and interrupted.

"There have been some new developments and I hope you understand that we are not at liberty to discuss anything fully. Please do not feel disrespected as we know you are concerned about the state of the business and all the lives that have been impacted. We just need to gather more information before we can fully disclose any findings."

"Of course. I can appreciate the need for discretion. Is there something I can do to assist, or do you need to use one of the offices or conference rooms today?" Kelly was not taken aback, and everyone could tell she had her heart in the correct place.

"We could use the records of the last two weeks of payroll transactions to include direct deposit and any paper checks which may have been issued. Also, the phone logs for any calls from the dispatchers and drivers for the last two weeks," Ronald was attempting to cover all driver bases as he did not want to disclose to Kelly that Quinn was the primary target of their visit.

"No problem. I can pull those up for you and bring them down to the conference room in less than thirty minutes, if you guys can wait." Kelly was already retrieving data from her computer as she spoke.

"Thanks sweetheart. You are the best and have always been the best. We will wait down in the first conference room down the hall," Jason smiled at Kelly and gently touched her on the shoulder as the two men made their way down the corridor to the conference room.

Once inside the conference room, the two made calls. Jason called his wife to check in with her and Ronald to his office to check in and see if there was any pressing business he needed to come by the office and assist with. The deputy assured him all was going well, and he wished Ronald success in wrapping up the investigation into the Staley case.

"Dude, you saved my ass back there. I am so new to this investigative stuff that I speak with my mouth in overdrive and my brain in neutral," Jason said.

"No harm done. I am sure Kelly is simply concerned and wants to help but until we can get a razor tight grip on this investigation and place Quinn Brown in handcuffs, I want as few people to know our plans as necessary. Any small slip of information could leak back to Quinn, and we need him to make a mistake and lead us to himself. Besides, I have been bailing your ass out of the fire for so long, it has become a normal reaction," Ronald said with a laugh.

Kelly brought the payroll and call logs down to the conference room in less than thirty minutes, as promised. She smiled at the men as she gently placed the paperwork down on the conference room desk and quickly slipped back outside the room and quietly closed the door.

Jason and Ronald began to scour the information. Jason was looking at the phone records as he would more readily be able to identify to whom the calls were placed and who made them. Ronald was checking over the payroll information and was able to see where Quinn's direct deposit had come back as unable to process. This was of course due to the block on his account. There were no paper checks issued. Ronald finished before Jason as there were several pages of phone calls placed due to Staley's being able to operate daily again. Although business had waned somewhat, customers were still loyal to the Staley's Trucking brand. Ronald slid his chair closer to Jason's and began to look at the calls as Jason very carefully scanned over each one. Ronald hoped to see some sort of pattern in the calls and hoped Quinn could be tracked by one or more of these calls. Jason would stare at a page for minutes on end and then flip it over and place it on another stack of checked pages. He did this for fifteen to twenty minutes and slowly reclined in his chair and rubbed his eyes and face with his hands as he exhaled deeply. He was turning to speak to Ronald when suddenly, he flipped the last page he had just viewed back over and began to run his finger down the list of calls. He looked up and smiled a wry smile at Ronald and pointed repeatedly at a cell number about halfway down the page.

"This is it. I think I know where this bastard is located," Jason was pointing at the number as if it should have some significance to Ronald, but Ronald was staring at him intently as if to ask him to elaborate.

Finally, Ronald spoke up. "What man? What the hell is up?"

"I went fishing with Quinn one afternoon several months ago and we were drinking a few beers and just enjoying the outdoors and friendly time together. We had had several beers, actually. He began to tell me things that an otherwise sober Quinn would have never shared. He talked about his childhood and what a tough time he had with his mother. She was an alcoholic and treated him and his brothers and sisters horribly. He went on to tell me she would slap them around for no apparent reason when she became drunk and how he wished she would simply drink herself to death and be out of his life. Quinn got his wish. When he was eighteen and he was the oldest of his four brothers and sisters, his mother died a horrible death from cirrhosis and liver failure. He talked for almost an hour without me saying a word. I could tell he needed to unload to someone, so I kept quiet and just drank beers along with him and listened in silence. He talked about his high school love; a lady named Renee. He said he never fell out of love with her, but they grew apart when she went to college, and he had to go to work to support himself and his brothers and sisters. Quinn said he met his future wife a few years later and she became pregnant, and he wanted to do the admirable thing and marry her. He still loved Renee but married his wife Kitty. He said he grew to love Kitty but never forgot about Renee. Fifteen years passed and he said he saw Renee. She had moved back to the metro Atlanta area after her divorce and was working for a law firm downtown. The two of them stayed in contact with each other and began to become closer with the passage of time. One thing led to another, and the friendship became physical. The two of them were meeting sometimes, as often as three times a week. Kitty became suspicious and hired a private detective to follow Quinn and the private investigator confirmed what Kitty knew in her heart. Kitty approached Quinn and told him to break the relationship off or she would take their three children and file for divorce. Quinn told me he still loved Kitty just not the way he loved Renee, but he did not want to lose his children. He broke off the relationship with Renee but never stopped loving her. He said they stopped seeing each other three years ago. When I finally spoke up and asked him how he contacted her without his wife seeing the calls on his cell phone bill, he explained that he bought a burner cell that only Renee had the number for. He explained he kept the burner cell phone as a backup in case his main cell was broken. He was so drunk that at this point he told me he would like me to have the number. I told him that was not necessary, but he insisted. I did not want to upset him, so I keyed the number into my cell phone. When I was scanning the paperwork just now, it took a second, but the number sprang into my head. It is such an odd number that even though I never used the number it resonated with me. The burner number is 404-867-5309. You know, Ronald, the classic 80's hit from Tommy Tutone. The song goes, 'Jenny, Jenny, I got your number, it's 867-5309'. "Jason was optimistic this was a huge clue for them.

"I'll be damned. Jason, who would have thought that your love of 1980's music and boring me nonstop with it on road trips, might be the biggest break in this case. I may buy you an 80's greatest hit CD collection, if this pays off.

"Let's reach out to Sheriff Powers and see if we can locate the area where the last call was placed from. It was only two days ago, and it looks like it was very brief. Less than a minute. It was a Saturday so he may have been trying to contact a person in the office who may be affiliated with the syndicate." Jason was highly optimistic at this point.

Ronald placed a call to a call to Sheriff Powers and Agents Wilkes and Wright. He knew the agents would have a broader scope of tracing methods, if Powers struck out on his end. They decided to go to Jason's house and let him see his family, wash and dry their clothes and have a home cooked meal. Ronald asked Jason to call Lindsey and see if she could fry up some of her famous fried chicken. They knew they may have to leave expeditiously, if Quinn's location could be pinpointed. They arrived at Jason's around 1:00 PM and Lindsey had prepared a huge lunch meal for the men. She handled their laundry as the two of them ate and then each fell asleep. Jason in his easy chair and Ronald stretched out on the sofa. Ronald's cell phone rang, and the two men leapt from their slumber. They thought it had only been twenty minutes or so since they drifted off, but it was now three hours later.

Ronald's call took only a couple of minutes, and he hung up and explained to Jason that the last call was late last evening, and it pinged from a cell tower near Cincinnati. Wilkes and Wright were working with agents in the area to pinpoint a more precise location. They were going to call them and Sheriff Powers once they knew something concrete.

Jason was shaking his head 'no' as Ronald spoke. "Call them back but ask them not to move forward until we arrive. I know exactly where he is. We need to get a flight to Cincinnati as soon as possible. They can secure the perimeter but please ask them to not move in until we arrive. I do not want to tip our hand and I think he would be more inclined to speak with me than anyone else. I will explain on the way to the airport. "

Ronald had already begun to search for flights on his cell phone. There was a direct flight leaving for Cincinnati in exactly ninety minutes. They had to hustle. Lindsey had already packed their clean clothing and was feeling eerily excited about this latest news. She kissed Jason goodbye, and he hugged his daughters. Ronald thanked her for the meal and the extended naptime, and they each raced out the door. Ronald would put on the lights and sirens on his cruiser to ensure they made it promptly to the airport and did not miss their flight.

On the way to the airport, Jason explained to Ronald that Renee had moved with her then husband to the Cincinnati area. He was an up-and-coming attorney and had secured a junior partnership with a firm there. Renee had no desire to live in downtown Cincinnati so she asked her husband if they could find a place in the suburbs. She had always been kind of a country girl at heart and Covington, Kentucky was across the John A. Roebling Suspension Bridge from the city limits of Cincinnati. It was only a two-mile drive to Cincinnati but to Renee it felt like one hundred miles difference. She told Quinn all about the decision and the day we went fishing/drinking he told me the story. When Renee got divorced, she asked for the country home she and her soon-to-be ex-husband had bought there years before. Her ex-husband had no desire to live there as he had fallen in love with the hustle and bustle of Cincinnati. Renee kept the property in Covington when she relocated to Atlanta and bought her small farm on the outskirts of Atlanta. Quinn must be there and awaiting an opportunity to disappear.

"Damn man. First 1980's music and now a drunken fishing trip. Your silly habits may just be the key to apprehending a felony.

They arrived at the airport, checked through TSA, and raced to their gate. The final boarding was just being called and they presented their tickets to the attendant. They boarded the aircraft and took their seats. The flight to Covington would take less than an hour and thirty minutes. It would be dark before they could arrive at Renee's property and would probably wait until daybreak to enter and search for Quinn. Ronald had received word that Wilkes and Wright had a team of agents surrounding the property and there was no possible way of entering or exiting without the team being aware.

CHAPTER 11

The Twists in Covington

Jason and Ronald were picked up at the airport by an agent from the Cincinnati division. He introduced himself as Special Agent Jonathan Kevin. Jonathan drove them to a secluded area on the outer perimeter of the Covington city limits. It was a beautiful area with Flowering Dogwood trees dotted the landscape and velvety, plush, green pastures as far as the eye could see. Agent Kevin turned down a small trail and turned off the ignition. Another agent approached the car from the brush ahead of them. The agent explained that the house in the distance was the property of Renee Gardner, once Mrs. Renee Felix. No one would be able to sleep this evening, and everyone kept glancing at their cell phones or watches anticipating the arrival of dawn.

The sun began to peek over the horizon at 5:45 AM. The agents had been in contact with each other throughout the night and were ready to move onto the property. Agent Kevin took the lead, along with Ronald and Jason. The cruisers quietly and slowly approached the home and surrounded the home and small barn on the backside of the main home.

The SWAT team from the Covington Police Department broke the door down and special agents, Covington Police, Sheriff's Deputies, and Ronald stormed inside the home. Jason, although deputized by Ronald, was asked to remain outside by Ronald's cruiser. You could hear calls of 'ALL CLEAR' throughout the upstairs and downstairs portions of the lovely, brick cottage home. After ten minutes and after the team had a second opportunity to scour each area of the home again, they moved towards the small, red painted barn which looked like something out of a Robert Frost poem. The barn had been surrounded, literally, by law enforcement agents awaiting the command to enter and search the structure. Several of the team which entered the home stayed back and surrounded the cottage in the event something was missed during the search inside, although this was highly improbable. The SWAT commander gave the command to enter the barn and to everyone's surprise Quinn Brown stood in the middle of the very well-manicured barn floor shaking uncontrollably and sobbing incessantly. One of the deputies moved forward quickly, but cautiously toward Quinn, with her weapon drawn and pointed at him. The deputy was less than five feet from Quinn when he suddenly pulled a snub nose .38 caliber pistol from his right-hand trouser pocket. The deputy slowly lowered her firearm and asked Quinn to place the weapon on the ground and back away from it. The other members of the law enforcement group kept their weapons raised and targeted towards Quinn.

"Hey Ronald. I recognize you. You're Jason's friend. How is Jason doing? He is a great guy and always treats me with respect. I remember telling him about me and Renee. I bet he thought about this place. He is a smart man," Quinn had lowered h head his almost a shameful manner as he spoke, sobbed, and it was obvious, struggling to focus.

"He is a great guy, and I know he would love to speak to you. I will send someone after him. He is right outside. It would be a lot easier for you guys to talk, if you let me hold your gun," Ronald said. He was very calm but concerned about where this situation could lead. He motioned for one of the SWAT members to go outside and retrieve Jason.

"This is a beautiful place, and your friend was awfully nice to let you stay here. How long have you been here? Is she here with you or nearby or any of your family?" Ronald was attempting to glean information and trying to win over Quinn's confidence simultaneously.

"No. No, just me. Kitty and the kids are at home and Renee is at her place. It is just me. I have done some bad shit and now will just be me forever," Quinn had again pressed the pistol against his temple and had begun to sob harder. He had lowered it by his waist earlier when Ronald first began to speak with him and had calmed somewhat.

Jason walked slowly into the barn area and smiled at Quinn. The deputy extended her arm to stop Jason from walking any closer to Quinn. Jason waved a small wave at Quinn and smiled again as he stopped alongside the deputy.

"Quinn, how are you? What's troubling you man? We have to sort through all this information and brush off our fishing gear and beer coolers and relax. Why don't you let me hold your pistol and you and I can sit down and have a damn beer right now. I always enjoyed our times together even though we didn't get to hook up very often." Jason walked a couple of paces toward Quinn and extended his hand toward Quinn asking for him to hand over the pistol. As he approached Quinn, the visible team members had lowered weapons in an attempt to lower the tension and see if it would help gain Quinn's confidence.

"Sorry, Jason. I can't hand over the pistol. Please step back and don't come any closer," Quinn said. He had pressed the pistol even harder against his temple to the point he had drawn blood, and it was trickling down the side of his head and down his cheek. When he did this the deputy closest to Jason grabbed him by his shirt and gently pulled him backwards and raised her weapon almost in unison with the remainder of the team. The smacking of the rifles and handguns resonated throughout the barn and sent out an eerie, almost deadly echo.

"Ok buddy. What can we do? What do you need from me? I want to help. You don't want to hurt yourself. Think about Kitty and your kids. Their graduations, sporting events at school, and giving away your daughter someday at her wedding. Don't do this man. Nothing good comes of this and anything that has happened in the past is not worth ruining your life and your family. Please let's talk," Jason was getting nervous as Quinn continued to rapidly slip into a mental state which everyone could sense was not healthy.

"I need you to accept my apologies and tell my family I love them. If you would, please tell Renee I have always loved her. Give my Christie away on her wedding day. I have done terrible shit and there is no coming back. This is the only way," Quinn had backed up a few steps and was now crying rivers of tears down both sides of his cheek. His right cheek was now a combination of tears and blood as they rolled down his face.

Jason stepped forward two paces and extended his hand again. As he was trying to draw closer and disarm Quinn. As Quinn allowed him to take another couple of steps closer without his moving backward, Jason felt he may be reaching him somehow. As Jason drew within two steps of Quinn and he had begun to think about the possibility of leaping out and tackling Quinn to the ground, Quinn took three rapid steps back, reached into his left trouser pocket, and tossed something at Jason's feet. Jason knew he had to act swiftly and as he prepared to lunge toward Quinn, a gunshot echoed like a clap of thunder throughout the barn. Jason had begun his leap almost simultaneously with Quinn's pulling of the trigger. Quinn fell to the ground and blood covered the left side of Jason's face and the front of his flannel shirt and blue jeans.

The SWAT and other officers moved in swiftly and Agent Kevin was on the radio requesting an ambulance to the farm's address. Ronald scooped up Jason and began to look him over to see if he had been struck by the bullet. The female deputy which had been close by the action all along had rolled Quinn over on his back and was about to attempt CPR. One of the SWAT members reached down and gently grabbed her by the left arm and pulled her to her feet. He reached down and checked for a pulse on Quinn's carotid artery on the left side of his neck. He mumbled loudly that an ambulance was not needed but the coroner's hearse would be. As Jason and Ronald stepped away from Quinn's body and let the SWAT members do their follow-up, they saw the object Quinn had tossed from his trouser pocket just before he shot himself.

Jason scooped up the carefully folded piece of paper and began to quickly unfold it. He stood there in silence and read what was written. Ronald had moved over beside him but could not read what was written. Jason read and reread the note for what seemed like an hour before he handed it over to Ronald. It was now Ronald's turn to read and read again the message written. He too took a couple of minutes to cover the contents. When he finally looked up from the note and stared over at Jason, it was not one of relief but one of confusion. The two men now stood in the center of the barn and all the radio chatter and conversations around them had not penetrated their hearing. They now stood there shaking their heads and mumbling under their breath.

"What in the hell do you make of this?" Ronald asked

"I'll be damned if I know. I would like to believe it is the truth, but I would also like to believe it is false because this means we may be no closer to the kingpin.

"Any evidence over here guys?" Agent Kevin walked up and stood between Jason and Ronald.

"This is a note Quinn tossed out of his trouser pocket just before he shot himself. I want to take a picture of it with my cell phone and I will turn it over to the Covington Sheriff's Office as evidence. I think when we get back to Georgia, we may have some loose ends to tie up and maybe even some more investigative work to do," Ronald spoke slowly as he pulled out his cell phone from his back pocket and snapped several pictures of the note before he handed it to Agent Kevin to tag as evidence.

Agent Kevin walked away and called out for one of the Covington deputies to come over and tag and bag the note for evidence. Ronald motioned for Jason to walk outside and the two of them made their way to an area outside the barn so they could speak privately. Ronald had to reach out and grab Jason as he continued walking after he had stopped. Jason was muttering under his breath and kicking a small rock he had seen at the entrance of the barn.

"This is nuts man. What the hell did he mean? Didn't he know his family could be protected and an answer from him could wrap this case up? Why all the damn secrecy?" Jason said. Obviously frustrated with the case.

"Let's look at this together and see if there is something we are missing," Ronald said. Reassuring Jason as he knew his friend was tired, angry, frustrated, and mentally and emotionally worn down.

Ronald opened the picture on his cell phone and enlarged the photo so both men could read it at the same time. The note read, 'Jason, I am sorry for all the undue stress this has caused you. I am sorry you were implicated but glad you are exonerated. As for me, I want you to know I have participated in horrific things, and I deserve to be punished. I am ashamed and do not deserve forgiveness for any of the things I have done. This is no excuse because I initially did it for the damn dirty money, but I was forced to continue to save my family. The head of all of this would slaughter them without so much as giving it a second thought. Even in death my family is not safe. I am sorry one final time, but I cannot disclose who the leader of this sick organization is. Jason, someday I hope you can forgive me'. Ronald closed the photo and put the phone back into his pocket. The two men stood staring at each other once again.

CHAPTER 12

Back to Georgia and Back to the New Normal

Jason and Ronald arrived back in Atlanta on the morning flight from Cincinnati. Ronald took Jason home and the two men stepped inside Jason's house for a cup of coffee and Ronald wanted to say hello to Lindsey. As was always Lindsey's practice, she had prepared the men a full breakfast along with their coffee. The girls were staying with their grandparents last night and today but would be home this evening to see their daddy. The three of them talked for nearly two hours over breakfast and more cups of coffee. Ronald and Jason explained to Lindsey what had transpired in Covington and how Quinn had committed suicide. They were sure there would be more loose ends to tie up but it seemed the two of them had done all they could do to help locate the syndicate leader and stop their illegal activities. Ronald thanked Lindsey for the fine meal and the conversation and headed toward the front door of the Jennings's home. It was time for him to return to Glynn County and assist his office with the workload there.

"Man, I knew you were a true friend, but this has been over and above. I will never be able to repay you. I love you and thank you my brother." Jason reached over and hugged his friend tightly as they leaned against Ronald's cruiser.

"Well, you know. What can I say? Having to save your ass is becoming so normal I don't even think about it anymore. I just accept it as my cross to bear. Dude, I love you and this family is just like my own. I am always here for you just as you are for me. I want you to come down to Brunswick and bring the kids. We will all take the boat out and do some shrimping. What is going on with Staley's? Are you going to continue to work there or are you going to try and catch on with another trucking company?"

"The news about Quinn was relayed to the two potential buyers and one of them was satisfied that the kingpin was now dead and there was no jeopardy of further instances with our trucking and warehouse team. They bought the business from the minority partners and Kelly said they were retaining everyone, keeping the name Staley's Trucking, and we could report as early as tomorrow. I will be going in tomorrow morning. The sooner I get this entire ordeal behind me, the better I will feel. I am still not convinced Quinn was the kingpin, but I am not convinced he was not. Kelly said the Atlanta Police felt he wrote that note in an attempt to clear his family and keep the police from digging deeper into their involvement. I truly believe they knew nothing about Quinn's involvement, and I believe they are innocent. I am so confused about this entire matter. I just want to be normal again."

"I understand the desire to be normal again. My gut tells me this was a dying declaration and Quinn was the man behind the operation. I wish he had given us more information on other people impacted by the trafficking. This was not ideal bonding time, but I did enjoy spending time with you. You almost became a deputy under my expert tutelage," Ronald said.

Jason enjoyed the time with his family that evening and the next morning. He left his home later than usual as he just missed his family and wanted those couple of extra hours with them. He arrived at what was now known as White's Trucking and Warehousing for accounting purposes but Staley's for operational purposes. Rube White was a lady who was a self-made millionaire and owned a chain of trucking and warehousing locations. She was a stern businessperson and was highly involved in the operations from the top-down. Rube was very generous to her employees, and she demonstrated that to everyone on this her day one as an owner. Every employee was given a five percent raise at the Atlanta location and a bonus for remaining with the organization after the acquisition. She met with the team as a whole that morning and laid out her expectations. Her meetings were always brief and to the point. She felt if the tires were not turning, we were not making money. Jason liked this approach as he liked the fact that he could show up for work, do his job well, be paid, and return home to his family. Jason received his first delivery assignment under the White Trucking umbrella. He was traveling to Little Rock and would drop a container there and return with a designated load from the White Trucking location there.

Ronald and Jason stayed in touch daily. Somehow this ordeal had impacted them in such a way that they realized that friendship was a gift and that they should never take it for granted. Jason told Ronald that he had spoken to Quinn's widow, Kitty, and their children. They were devastated and embarrassed by his death and actions with the syndicate. They expressed their love for him and would try to remember him as a husband and dad and not a malicious criminal. He also mentioned that he located a number for Renee and told her about Quinn and how he felt about her. She thanked Jason but asked that he not reach back out to her as she needed to put Quinn and anyone associated with him behind her.

Life went along like this for the two friends for the next six months. Jason took the family down to Jekyll Island and as promised, Ronald took them out on his boat for a couple days of shrimping the beautiful Atlantic waters. The days on the road delivering containers again helped to return Jason back to normalcy and reestablish his routine. He loved being a husband and daddy. It was his life. Ronald, who never really admitted to anyone, and certainly not himself, was shaken by the search for Quinn Brown and needed to reestablish himself and his routine, as well. Pushing forward in the new normal.

CHAPTER 13

Another Discovered Trafficking

It was early one Tuesday morning at a truck stop outside of Denver. The driver of the rig had stopped overnight as he was experiencing some form of an odd vibration in his engine and did not want to risk as breakdown along Interstate 70, so he pulled into the closest truck stop which was adjacent to Class 8 (large semi transport) repair shop. His name was Stephen Crowley. Stephen had made a pickup in Canada the afternoon before and was due in Salt Lake City by this afternoon. This emergency stop would not allow him to be there and make his appointment time. He called his dispatcher in Savannah and told them about his issue and asked that they call the customer and inform them the container would not be delivered until at least Wednesday morning. Stephen decided to have an early breakfast at the diner located on the truck stop grounds as the repair shop would not be open for another hour. He ate his breakfast and surfed the internet on his cell phone and decided to make his way back to his rig and attempt to be the first in line for service at the repair shop. As he walked slowly beside his container examining the tires for any damage, he heard something tapping on the inside of the container. He tapped loudly on the outside of the container in the vicinity of where he thought the tapping from the inside was happening. He thought maybe some of the freight had shifted and the pallet was bumping against the inside of the container. As he tapped multiple times, he could not feel any resistance against the container wall and no longer heard any noise. He chalked the noise up to his imagination and went back to the business of examining the tires for damage and wear. As he was checking the last of the chassis tires, he heard the same tapping again and this time a little more forceful. Stephen called out to see if a voice may be on the other side of the container, but he received no response. This was a little more disturbing than he cared for and decided to yield on the side of caution. He searched for the nearest DOT office in the area and called the customer service line. The representative asked Stephen to stay with the container and do not move it. They would like to have a DOT Officer dispatched immediately to assist him. Stephen did as he was asked and in less than twenty minutes a DOT cruiser came racing toward his rig with lights flashing and sirens wailing. Stephen walked toward the cruiser as he came to a rest fifteen feet behind his container. A slender, very attractive DOT Officer made her way out of the cruiser and walked briskly up to Stephen.

"Good morning, my name is Officer Darlene Bennett. Are you Stephen Crowley?

"Good morning, officer. I am Stephen Crowley. I heard a noise inside container and dismissed it as freight suddenly shifting inside and bumping the interior of the container. I went about my inspection of the chassis tires as I was about to take my rig across the street to the repair shop and have an engine noise investigated and repaired, if needed. As I was wrapping up the tire inspection, I heard tapping from the inside again and I called out, but no one answered. I am not authorized to remove the CTPAT seal but I felt as if I should engage the DOT for assistance." Stephen was a little nervous as he watched Darlene scribble furiously on her notepad and had begun to record the conversation with her cell phone.

"Better to be safe than sorry. I am going to record the CTPAT seal number and capture a picture of it. I can place a new seal on the trailer for you once we verify everything is in order and checked out. Please get your manifest, license, and registration so I can fill out the necessary forms and begin." Darlene said.

She popped the latch with her key fob and retrieved a set of bolt cutters from the trunk. She quickly walked back to the rear of the container where Stephen was standing at the ready with his license, manifest, and registration, as requested. Darlene took the information and began writing a report of the incident and the necessity to remove the CTPAT seal. She had written up the report in just a few minutes and was wrapping the cutters around the seal to sever it and enter the container. She picked up the seal and placed it in a plastic bag to ensure chain of custody. She swung the doors open and climbed inside the container. She motioned for Stephen to climb inside and asked that he turn on his cell phone flashlight. She had a flashlight positioned on her gun belt and had begun to swing the light left to right along the inside of the container. The manifest stated that the container was loaded with automobile windshields and were all either palletized or placed inside metal racking designed to safely transport the glass merchandise. The pallets were not very wide, and a person could walk carefully around them to reach the front of the container. Darlene took the right side and Stephen the left. They meticulously made their way toward the front of the container and were shining light on every inch of space in front of them and around themselves. About three-fourths of the way inside the container, Stephen bumped into something and shined his cellular phone light over the object. He discovered it to be a black body bag and it had a stomach-churning stench. His heart began to race, his throat dried up, and he was breathing deep, frightened breaths.. He tried to call out to Officer Bennett but could not form words. He banged loudly on the side of the container to get her attention. She abruptly swung the light in his direction and the light temporarily blinded him. He regained his composure and motioned for her to come to his location. Darlene quickly navigated a path through the center of the container and arrived where Stepehen was standing in just moments. She shined the light down in the direction of Stephen's cell phone light and looked down at the object and then quickly back at him.

"What in the name of heaven can this be? I need you to take my flashlight and hold it steadily on the object," Officer Bennett was carefully handing over the flashlight to Stephen as she was simultaneously removing her weapon from the holster.

"Ah, ok," Stephen was able to dryly respond as he reached a shaking hand over toward the flashlight and grabbed it nervously.

He was trying to hold the light steady as Officer Bennett knelt and began to slowly unzip the black bag. When she had unzipped the bag as far as it would go, she flipped the bag open and there lay a young woman no more than twenty or twenty-one years old with her feet and hands bound and duct tape over her mouth. The stench the two of them smelled was the urine and excrement which had flowed from the young women, down the leg of her jeans and settled in the bottom of the bag. She was a very lovely young woman with dark black hair and a lovely figure. Darlene gently removed the duct tape from her mouth and cut the ropes from the woman's hands and legs. She stood the lady up against the wall of the container and motioned for Stephen to put the lady's right arm over his shoulder as she had positioned her left arm over her shoulder to assist her out of the container.

The two of them moved as swiftly as they possibly could and navigated their way to the rear of the container. Stephen wrapped both arms around the lady and held her upright as she limply leaned on him in her unconscious state. Officer Bennett had begun to climb down from the container and motioned for Stephen to hand the lady down to her on the ground. Stephen bent down and carefully handed the lady down to Darlene. Darlene wrapped both of the lady's arms around her neck and made her way to the back of her cruiser. She opened the door and gently laid the lady down on the backseat of her cruiser. Stephen had jumped out of the back of the container and was now standing by the opened back door of the DOT cruiser. Darlene was on her cell phone calling an ambulance to the location. She then immediately called her office and requested local police backup and her supervisor from the DOT Office.

The ambulance arrived in less than ten minutes. The two rescue team members loaded the lady on a gurney and placed her in the back of the ambulance. She was alive but in a seriously dehydrated and lacking nutrition state. Minutes after the ambulance arrived, three Denver Police Officers arrived and Darlene's supervisor from the DOT. Stephen and Darlene told the officers how he had heard the noise and called the DOT for assistance. They went on to explain how they had found the young woman and moved as swiftly as they could to get her emergency medical attention. The officers roped off the area and asked that Darlene and Stephen stay with them as they handled their investigation as they felt they may have more questions to ask. As they waited, Stephen called his dispatcher and told them about his situation and that they would need to let the customer know that their container was on an indefinite hold by the Denver Police Department.

The police finished their investigation in a couple of hours. They informed Stephen that he would have to drive the container to their impound yard where it would be kept until further notice. The police deduced that the young woman must have heard Stephen outside the container and in hopes that he was not part of the people who had kidnapped her used her last conscious moments to kick at the container wall. It was a last-ditch effort to save herself and God had to have been on her side this morning. Stephen drove the trailer to the police impound yard and dropped it where he was instructed. He then drove the truck back to the repair shop as the engine vibration had become more pronounced. The shop was closing as it was after 5:00 PM now. Stephen asked if he could park outside and sleep in the cab of his rig and get a mechanic to look at the truck first thing the next morning. The shop gladly allowed him to and told him they would handle his repair first thing tomorrow morning. Stephen went back to the small diner and had a light dinner. He returned to his rig and decided to call it an early evening and try to get some rest.

The story of the young woman being found in the container made national news, of course. It was all over the evening news, newspapers, and social media. The police were hoping someone might have a clue or come forward with any information which might prove helpful. Both Jason and Ronald saw the story on the internet and each of the men had the same eerie thought. Could this be the same syndicate pulling off this trafficking? It was from Canada, but where? Surely not from the Windsor location. Ronald called Jason early Wednesday morning and asked if he saw the story. Jason told him he saw it and had thought of nothing else but the incident all night and morning. Ronald told him he was going to reach out to Special Agents Wilkes and Wright to see what their thoughts were and if they could share any additional information with him. Jason told Ronald he had to make a quick delivery to Birmingham today but would have his cell phone with him and call him as soon as he knew something. Both men shared their concern with each other on how they felt this was no coincidence and they feared the trafficking from Windsor may have been renewed.

Jason had made his delivery to Birmingham and was backing underneath the container which would be returning to Atlanta with him. As he was outside hooking up his air hoses and checking the chassis tires for damage, his cell phone rang. It was Ronald. Ronald asked if he was driving, and Jason explained he was just hooking up the container for the return trip to Georgia. Ronald told Jason he had spoken to Agent Wilkes for over an hour and a half, and she laid out some information on the lady found in Denver and confirmed some thoughts the two of them had. Ronald went on to explain that the container had indeed originated at a warehouse outside of Windsor but not the warehouse Rowland Davis had been affiliated with. The young girl in Denver was a twenty-one-year-old who had been on the run from an abusive ex-boyfriend. Her name was Jayla Gobert. She was a French speaking citizen of Windsor and had been living parttime in a halfway house for abused women. Wilkes and Wright were en route to Denver when they saw the news about Jayla as they had the same inclinations that we did. They are going to speak with her tomorrow as she has regained consciousness but is still at a local Denver hospital to recover. Ronald stated he was going to wait to hear back from the agents and promised to call Jason immediately when he heard back from them. Jason thanked Ronald for the call and told him he should be back in Atlanta in less than three hours. He would be at home with Lindsey and the girls.

Jason had a smooth drive from Birmingham to Atlanta. He had left his pickup truck at Staley's Trucking. He decided to park the container and his rig on the lot at Staley's and drop the trailer tomorrow, if he had a load to haul. It was about 5:30 PM when he arrived at Staley's and as he expected, he saw Kelly's car in her parking spot in front of the office. Jason decided to run in and speak to his favorite secretary and see how her day had gone. Kelly was made up beautifully and dressed to perfection and the smile still lights up the room. She was hammering away on her computer and finishing up a call when Jason walked up to her desk.

"What's happening young lady? Do you ever stop working? All the guys you have chasing you, I would think you would be heading home for a nice dinner date." Jason smiled at Kelly as she blushed a bit at the compliments.

"No. it will just be me, my puppy, and a Netflix movie tonight. How was your day? We have something for you tomorrow, if you are interested in running. I was just curious. Did Ronald hear anything about that young girl out in Denver? I saw it all over the news. I felt like he would reach out and see what he could find out. Do you know if it is the same group who Quinn was affiliated with? I just pray this group and can caught and shut down permanently," Kelly had begun to tear up a little as she spoke.

"I spoke with Ronald, and he made some calls but nothing concrete. I am in the same boat as you are. I hope like hell they nail these bastards that are doing this to these women and put them under the jail. I can't imagine the horror these women have faced and if they will ever get over the experience. I am sorry. I went off track there. I just wanted to say hello and see how you were. Go home little lady and watch your Netflix." Jason said.

I will. I promise I will be leaving here in the next ten minutes. Thanks for stopping by. You are a sweet man Jason and a good friend. You care about people and that is a lost art in this world and time," Kelly said.

Jason turned and walked out of the office and to his pickup truck. He was ready for a hot shower and dinner and an early night to bed with Lindsey. He fired up the truck and headed home. He continually thought about the young lady in Denver and hoped Wilkes and Wright could unearth some answers and bust this sickening syndicate.

CHAPTER 14

A New Set of Suspects

The next morning Jason arose early and had breakfast with Lindsey. He and Lindsey had stayed up later than they wanted to with the girls, but Jason never could say no to time with his three ladies. He kissed Lindsey and made his way out the front door of their home and out to his pickup truck. As he was getting ready to fire up the ignition, his cell phone rang. It was Ronald. Jason turned the truck off and stepped outside to answer the call. He propped himself up against the back bed of the pickup and answered the call.

"What the hell are you doing other than wasting the taxpayers of Glynn County's cash? Do they know how much you get paid not to accomplish a damn thing?" Jason said.

"They told me if I kept having to save your ass that Lindsey would have to put me on her payroll because it was becoming a fulltime job. How are you doing buddy? Good morning to you."

"I am good, my friend. Please tell me Wilkes and Wright have some news for us," Jason said.

"Are you sitting down? This may take a minute but here goes. I want your thoughts on something. I know this is going to sound like I am off the reservation but hear me out."

"At this point, Ronald, I would settle for any type of lead or fresh idea."

"I know this may seem a little far fetched or even maybe a little cruel but after I spoke with Agents Wilkes and Wright, I got to thinking to myself about an impossible twist that just will not settle in my gut. So, I called Agent Wilkes back with my thoughts and she made a couple of phone calls. Her contacts have access to more information and can get answers a lot more quickly than my office can. It turns out my hunch was right, or at least partially right. The Dupont family adopted those young girls we met several months ago. Pierre has contacts with the RCMP, and he and Anna have worked with adoption agencies within Canada to adopt the girls. This is where my thinking gets twisted, and I pray that I am wrong about this. If you recall, when we arrived at their home Pierre and Anna left the room and said something in French to the girls. Of course, you and I did not understand what he was saying, and we really didn't think too much about it. I noticed the girls did not respond but only nodded a confirmation toward Pierre. They were all very stern in their appearance and were visibly shaken at the time. I understand they had not long been through a horrifying experience but in hindsight I wonder if they were intimidated or even afraid of Pierre and Anna."

"I don't get where you are going. Why would these girls fear Pierre and Anna? They adopted them and gave them homes. Pierre also sent us the point of contact with the RCMP to help with the investigation at Windsor," Jason said.

"I get that Jason but hear me on this. I know it sounds cruel, but it just will not go away. Pierre and Anna also have adoption contacts. I asked Agent Wilkes to see if they were engaged in any other philanthropic activities in the last several years. She found out Anna and Pierre were once a safehouse which was one of several homes which served as halfway houses for runaways and abused women."

"I'll be damned. Jayla was living in a halfway house before she was found in Denver. This is making a lot more sense now.

Wilkes was unable to find out why they suspended their involvement in the halfway house operation, and everyone just believed they had adopted the children and were busy taking care of them. If the Dupont Family used their connections with the halfway houses to find out who was there and under what circumstances and then Pierre used his buddies with the RCMP to cover up activities and implicate people like Rowland Davis and Quinn Brown as the bad guys, then they look like saints and angels. A little thin but what do you think?"

"If they are the kingpins, why wouldn't one of the girls take a risk by telling us or someone else?"

"The Dupont family could have them killed and even kill their sisters. Pierre spent a lot of time detailing how their families were slaughtered in front of the girls that day we were at their home. Why would he dredge that old memory up and why do it in front of the girls. He could have asked us to step into the kitchen or outside and shared that story with us. I think it was to further frighten the girls into telling us what Pierre and Anna had prepared as the truth. One last thing was troubling me. You remember how the girls could not understand the word the kidnapper was using when he was speaking French? I know they were frightened, and people do not always understand what others are saying but it seemed like they were retelling a prepared response to me and not someone who was trying to recall what word the kidnapper used. A lot of coincidences but my law enforcement gut feeling just will not let this go Jason."

"Wow! Let's say all of this is correct and the Dupont family are the kingpins in this operation, how in the hell do we prove all of this. If we cannot get one of the girls or the RCMP to collaborate some or all of this, we can't prove Pierre and Anna have been anything but angels of mercy."

"I think it is time we take a trip back to Quebec and see if we can speak with one of the girls away from the Dupont home and see if they are less reluctant to talk away from Pierre and Anna. How soon can you leave?" Ronald asked.

"I have a run going somewhere today. Let me call the office and see if the dispatcher can arrange for another driver to deliver. I will call you back in five minutes and let you know. If they can deliver my container, I can meet you at the airport in an hour. "

Jason called the dispatcher office number at Staley's Trucking, and it rang several times. He knew it was early for anyone to be there but was hopeful one of the dispatchers had arrived early. After the seventh or eighth ring, Jason had given up hope of reaching anyone and thought he would drive into the office and speak with someone when they arrived. Just as he was about to end the call on his cell phone, a soft, sweet voice answered saying 'Good morning. Staley's Trucking.' Jason recognized the voice. It was Kelly. She was always there. When did this lady sleep, he thought to himself?

"Good morning, sunshine. How is your day? I need a favor, please."

"Good morning, Jason. Anything for you. What can I help you with?"

"I need to see if there is someone who can handle my container delivery today. I know you said I had one lined up, but I need to cancel it and any upcoming for a few days, if possible, please."

"Of course, Jason. I will have the dispatchers change some things around when they arrive this morning and cover everything. Are Lindsey and the girls, ok? You aren't sick, are you?"

"No, I am fine, and so are Lindsey and the girls. Ronald and I need to check on something pertaining to the lady found at the Denver truck stop location. We should not be, but a couple of days and I will handle whatever loading you guys need. I appreciate you all being flexible with me. Let Mrs. Rube know that I am extremely sorry, and I will make up for the times I have missed and then some, if she will only bear with me for a few more days."

"Mrs. Rube knows how pivotal you are to her operation, and she understands why you are doing what you are doing. Are you guys flying back out to Denver? Do you need me to book you and Ronald a flight?" Kelly asked.

"No thanks I am sure Ronald will handle the bookings for us. We are actually heading back to Quebec. There are some loose ends to tie up there and that is why I need to additional time away. I promise to only be away less than four or five days, and I will be back to work full blast," Jason was appreciative in his response and felt gratitude for all of Kelly's concern.

Jason hung up with Kelly and immediately called Ronald to let him know he was free to leave anytime and would meet him at the airport. Lindsey had already packed Jason a bag when he made his way back inside their house. She had stepped outside to see why he had not left yet after she saw him standing in the driveway for such a long time. She had eavesdropped on his conversation and Jason was so immersed in the call that he did not realize she was standing less than twenty feet away. He grabbed the bag and kissed his wife goodbye. He told her hoped to be back in four or five days and would call each day to let her know how they were doing. He jumped in the driver's seat and fired up his pickup.

He had to meet Ronald at the airport in three and half hours and he was not sure how the morning traffic would be flowing and he wanted to grab lunch at one of the restaurants there, also. He arrived at the airport and Ronald had just landed from his flight departing from Brunswick. It was a short forty-minute flight, and he called Jason to let him know what gate to meet him at. Jason checked through TSA and headed for the departing gate for Quebec. Ronald had already sat down at the restaurant closest to their flight gate and was having a cheeseburger. Jason sat down with his friend and ordered himself a burger and the two men rehashed the new developments and ideas Ronald had shared earlier in the day. Jason finished his burger, and the men headed to have a seat in front of their departure gate. The flight was on time, and they entered the plane and took their seats. Neither man would admit it, but they both hoped they were wrong about Pierre and Anna.

Chapter 15

Quebec Answers Some but Not All

The flight into Quebec was a smooth one and touched down around 6:00 PM local time. Ronald and Jason decided to check into a hotel, have dinner, and get a very early start the next day. They were not going to alert Pierre and Anna of their visit as they did not want to allow them to prepare for the visit or intimidate the adopted daughters in any way. The plan was to get the oldest daughter, Celine, alone and try to get her to open more and perhaps shed light on Ronald's theory. Agent Wilkes had also agreed to accompany the men to the Dupont home. She felt as if having a lady there may make Celine more inclined to talk to her and share everything she may know.

Agent Wilkes had arrived in Quebec ahead of Jason and Ronald. She had checked into the same hotel the men had and wanted to have dinner with them and discuss a plan forward for tomorrow morning. The men checked in, freshened up a bit, and met Madison, as she asked the men to call her, at the hotel café for dinner. Madison was already at the café bar having a cocktail when Jason and Ronald arrived downstairs. She grabbed her drink and followed them to the table the hostess had given them. The three of them ordered dinner and discussed how they would proceed tomorrow morning after a quick breakfast at this same café.

The next morning all three of them arrived at the café at 5:45 AM. It was set to begin serving breakfast at 6:00 AM and they wanted to be first to order so they could be on their way to the Dupont home. They rode together in Agent Wilkes car as the men had taken a cab from the airport. Madison asked the men to remain in the car until she had an opportunity to speak with Pierre and Anna and ask permission to see Celine. Madison told the men she would say it was just a quick follow up to finish her report on the matter as she felt this part of the investigation for the United States was complete.

They pulled up in front of the Dupont home at 7:00 AM and Madison exited the car and made her way up the driveway to the front door. She rang the bell as Jason and Ronald sat in the car which had been parked one house over and across the street in hopes the men would not be visible to anyone answering the door at the Dupont home. Madison wanted this to go smoothly. After a few seconds, the door swung open, and Charlotte stood in the doorway. Madison introduced herself, showed Charlotte her badge and credentials, and asked if Mr. and Mrs. Dupont were home. Charlotte shook her head 'no' and Madison asked if she could come in. Charlotte allowed her to come inside and offered her a seat on the sofa.

"Are your sisters home today? I would like to speak with all of you, if I possibly could. I heard everything about you all from my friends from Georgia, Mr. Ronald and Mr. Jason. They say you are all very beautiful, sweet, and smart. I can see they were absolutely correct," Madison was trying to put the young girl at ease.

"They are here. Let me go get them. Please wait here." When she stepped into the back of the house, Madison grabbed her cell phone and quickly texted Ronald to ask them to stay inside the car and she would get them as soon as she felt it was comfortable with the girls. Within a couple of minutes, two other girls emerged from the bedrooms at the rear of the home. Along with Charlotte, were now her sisters Celine and Camille. The three of them sat down on the easy chair which their daddy Pierre usually sit. Celine in the chair and Charlotte and Camille on each of the arms of the chair. Madison introduced herself and once again showed her credentials to all three girls to set their minds at ease.

"Where is Mr. and Mrs. Dupont? Will they be home soon? I really wanted to speak with you girls but also wanted to see your parents. I am here to ask a few follow-up questions about the incident in Texas. Do you all remember speaking to Mr. Ronald and Mr. Jason? I am their friend and trying to help them arrest the people responsible for your kidnapping."

Celine spoke up. "We remember both of them. They were very nice men and Mr. Jason tried to help us back in Texas. Papa Pierre and Mama Anna are gone with our sister Louise. I am not sure when they will return or if ever, they will return."

Madison texted Ronald quickly and asked the two men to come inside. "Mr. Ronald and Mr. Jason are right across the street and would like to talk with you, if that is ok. What do you mean 'if they ever return'? They didn't indicate that they would be back later today. Do you have a number I can reach them at?" Madison was reaching for her cell phone when there was a gentle knock on the front door.

Camille went to the front door and saw Jason and Ronald. She let them both inside and Charlotte went with her into the kitchen to get two chairs for them to sit in. They returned with the chairs and Ronald and Jason took a seat. Jason spoke to the girls and smiled broadly at them. The girls smiled at him, hugged him, and returned to their seats on the easy chair and arms.

"The girls were just telling me that Mr. and Mrs. Dupont have left for the day. Celine said she wasn't sure when they would be back. She was about to tell me why she thought they may not return at all," Madison was filling the men in on the information shared while at the same time not trying to raise the level of concern in the room. She wanted the girls to tell their story in their way and time.

Celine began to speak again and as she spoke a small tear trickled down her cheek. "Papa and Mama gathered us together in the living room this morning before daybreak. It was possibly 4:00 AM. They stated they had to leave and take Louise with them. We asked if we could go, and they said 'no'. Mama hugged and kissed us and said she was sorry and hoped we would understand after we read the letter. Papa hugged and kissed us each as did Louise. Louise stood sobbing uncontrollably and did not say anything. They each had two suitcases each and loaded them all in the car. Papa handed us this note and he left without another word to us. We understand what he meant by the note but are not sure why these things happened. There was $1,500 Canadian Dollars in the envelope with the note. I am not sure what my sisters and I will do now."

At this point all three girls were crying and could not be consoled.

"May we see the note, please. Is it in French or English?" Jason gently extended his hand to take the note from Celine.

"It is in French. I can translate for you," Celine said.

Jason looked and it and passed it to Ronald and then Ronald to Madison. Madison took a picture of the note with her cell phone and then began to type the contents of the note into her translator app on her phone. She looked up and at Celine and asked her to tell them what the note said and what she thought her parents might mean by the note.

Celine took a deep breath and slowly began. "The note says that we three need to know that Mama and Papa love us very much. Louise loves us, as well. We were never stepsisters or adopted children. We were real sisters and children in their hearts. They had to leave and try to disappear and start a new life. They had been forced to do some evil things for some even more evil people. We would need to take this money and get away or find Mr. Ronald or Mr. Jason for help. They did not do these things for money or for greed but to protect Louise. They have come to realize protecting one at the sacrifice of others was no longer worth it and knew the demands would never stop. They wrote again that they loved us and please do not try to contact them or locate them as it was best this way."

"Where would they go? Do you girls have any idea? Have you tried their cell phones? It would be best if we speak to them." Ronald was calm but there was a sense of urgency in his voice.

"The cell phones are in the bedrooms. I am sure they have burner cell phones now and we do not have the numbers. I can tell you what I know, but I need to speak to you alone," Celine was still crying as she looked softly at her sisters as if to ask them to leave the room. The two sisters stood up slowly and walked to the farthest bedroom in the rear of the home and gently closed the door.

"Can I get you something to drink? Some water, perhaps?" Madson asked as she had finished translating the note on her phone and was attempting to calm Celine.

"No. I am fine. I did not want my sisters to hear. They would never understand. Papa told me things right before we were taken and he said I would be strongest and understand as I was the oldest. Papa was approached by someone almost two years ago. I am not sure how they knew or who may have told them, but they knew Papa had adopted us. The person told Papa that he would need to hand over my sisters and me in exchange for them not kidnapping and trafficking Louise. Papa refused but a few days later there was a picture in our mailbox of Louise and two men walking behind her as she was coming home from school. There was a note attached to the picture saying that he had two days to turn us over to them or Louise would be taken. Papa told me he made a most vile deal with the men. He told them he knew of two young girls set to be adopted and where they could be found in the foster homes. Papa said he would never have provided that information to them, but he was shown pictures of where our dads were killed and of our mothers being loaded in a container to be sold. He knew they would take Louise and us and maybe even kill him. He knew that was no excuse, but he was not thinking clearly. The two girls disappeared and have never been located. Papa knew what had happened to them. The people came back months later and Papa refused to provide any further information. The next day Louise was kidnapped and the only way to ransom her was for Papa to turn one of us over to the traffickers. Papa told me what they had done, and I asked him to please ensure I was with Charlotte and Camille as I could try to protect them, and they would not be as afraid. This was more than those evil devils could have dreamed of. They now had three of us. We were placed on the container in Windsor and taken to Georgia where your Quinn Brown was to take us to Texas, but things worked out where Mr. Jason was the driver of that container. Thank God, he found us and saved us." Celine was now crying so hard that she could barely speak clearly.

"The first time we were here, you mentioned that one of the men said something like 'la folle or le fou'. Was that really what they said? I can't seem to shake the idea that you, being a native French speaker, did not understand what they were saying." Ronald had pulled his notes from the previous visit and was scanning them quickly.

"Papa instructed me to say that. He was threatened once again and was told by this group that if we gave them any information other than that of Rowland Davis, we would all be executed. I heard them clearly say 'la reine' not 'la folle'. La reine is French for the queen. La folle means crazy or insane in our language. The man clearly said 'la reine'. "

'What does 'la reine' mean?" Madison was translating it on her phone but wanted Celine's native definition?

"La reine, means queen, in your language. The head of this satanic group is a woman. How could a woman do such things to other human beings and especially other women," Celine was so exhausted from her tears and reliving the last year that she sank back into the chair and buried her head into her hands?

"The first thing we must do, is get you and your sisters to safety. I want you to be in the United States as I am not sure how deep this may run in the RCMP. I hope Mr. Dupont didn't use any undue influence over them, but we can't take any chances with you and your sister's lives." Madison was dialing Special Agent Wright as she spoke.

Madison would escort the three sisters back to the USA and place them in protective custody. The new identities and life could perhaps put this nightmare behind them. Celine would have the most difficulty as she had been entrusted with some painful and life altering information. She would survive and bounce back but at what cost and what length. Ronald, Jason, and Madison stood by while the three girls packed and would drive them to the airport. Agent Wright had made flight arrangements for them, and they would be in an undisclosed location by the following morning. The six of them arrived at the airport. Madison asked Ronald and Jason to bring her luggage back to Georgia and she would arrange to pick it up in the near future. Celine, Charlotte, and Camille all hugged and kissed Jason and hugged Ronald. The three girls said their goodbyes and Madison walked with them into the airport.

Jason looked at Ronald intently. "Now what my friend?"

"Well. We take our asses back to the hotel, get something to eat, go to bed, and go back to Georgia tomorrow. Madison and Agent Wright have new leads and are going to get Celine and her sisters in a safe place so they can perhaps rebuild their lives and have a future. You go back to hauling freight and I go back to Glynn County and catch some local bad guys. You should be proud Jason. You worked hard, helped catch some criminals, and changed the course of three young girls' lives. Now you get to go back to Atlanta and be with your three girls. I am honored to call you friend," Ronald hugged his friend and patted him heartily on the back.

"We helped these girls and helped bust Davis's ass, but I wish we had caught this person. If you can call her a lady, this sick, twisted lady. You saved my butt and were with me all through this man. I truly am grateful." Jason and Ronald hailed a taxicab and headed for the hotel.

Chapter 16

Wilkes and Wright on the Trail

J ason was back in less than four days as promised and was back on the job at Staley's Trucking. He thought often of the journeys he and Ronald had been through the past several months and how he wished the kingpin, or in this case, lady could be caught and prosecuted. His girls were growing like weeds and he and Lindsey had even begun to talk about adding to their family. Lindsey knew he loved his daughters with all his heart, but she knew deep down Jason longed for a son.

Ronald was coming up for reelection in November. It would be a landslide victory for him as it had been the other two times he had run but he still worried. His girlfriend was his biggest cheerleader and ensured him she would be on the campaign trail with him. Everyone in Glynn County knew he had tirelessly pursued the innocence of his friend and the persons behind the trafficking ordeal. He was Glynn's favorite son and deep inside he knew the county loved him. He stayed in touch with Agent Wilkes, and she kept him as up to date as she could due to confidential information as she could. Some things were off limits, knowing that he had stepped away from the case, but Wilkes knew he could be trusted and was concerned so she let him know what she could. Ronald and his girlfriend had begun to think about the next step in their relationship and decided on a wedding date after Ronald surprised her a month after he arrived back home from Quebec with a diamond engagement ring.

One Friday night, Ronald was about to call Jason and see if he was home and ask if they would like to drive down the next morning and take the boat out off the Jekyll Island coast. As he was reaching for his cell phone on the edge of the sofa, a text popped in. Agent Wilkes asked him to call her when he had a few minutes. Ronald immediately dialed her number as he was anxious to see what she had to say.

Madison answered on the second ring. "Good evening, Ronald. I have some potentially good news to share, and I may need your help. We have located Pierre and Anna Dupont, and they have agreed to be charged with trafficking crimes and aiding and abetting, if we can secure protection for their daughter, Louise. I have my notes from our trip to Quebec and discussion with Celine, but I was wondering if I might review yours. I know you shared everything with us, but I would like to talk with you and Jason, if possible, and see if there may be anything you might remember that we did not document. "

"This is great news. Hell yes. Where do you need us and when? Where did they find the Duponts?

"I will get the details together on where and when we need to meet and let you know on Monday. We have something s to iron out with the Canadian government on jurisdictional items, but I do not believe they are going to fight us on extradition. They feel they have the most solid case and the testimony of his adoptive daughters who are now living and acquiring their United States citizenship. Please gather all your notes and I think, at first glance, it will be easier for Agent Wright and I to meet you guys in Atlanta. If Jason could just let his work know and handle local runs that would be great. He doesn't need to let anyone know we are coming as this is now, we hope, getting closer to pinpointing a suspect leader. The fewer who know, the better. I will call you Monday morning and hopefully we can all be in Atlanta on Tuesday. Pierre and Anna were found in a small town called Yarmouth, Nova Scotia. Wright leaned on the RCMP and one of Pierre's old running buddies was still employed with them and gave them Yarmouth as a possible hiding spot. The old friend turned out not to be such a happy friend. Pierre apparently stole Anna away from him years ago and the guy never got over it. He said he had also been trying to save for over ten years to buy a vacation cottage in Yarmouth and Pierre came swooping in at the last minute and offered more money for the property. He said Pierre and Anna used to vacation there often and spoke about the town occasionally to sort of rub the property in his face. It didn't take much arm twisting from Wright to get the information. We staked out the city with about ten agents. It did not take long to spot them. The town has less than 10,000 people living there. It was like shooting fish in a barrel after we arrived.

"I will let him know and we will keep everything confidential. Thanks for calling me. This is exciting. I am reserving full-blown excitement but excited still. This could be our big break and you and Wright deserve the credit.

Ronald hung up with Madison and immediately called Jason. He was half asleep on the sofa and the call startled him. Ronald told Jason everything Madison had shared with him, and he asked Jason not to say anything to anyone, including Lindsey. Ronald knew she could be trusted but he knew Wilkes would never bring him into her circle of trust again, if he blew this opportunity. Jason assured him there would be no one else told and if he had to take sick time away from work to explain his absence, he would do that. Jason too was excited but dared not express it, as he knew Lindsey would be curious. He just told her that it was Ronald and was talking about the big upcoming wedding which still did not have a firm date.

Jason received a call from Ronald mid-morning on Monday. Wilkes and Wright would be coming down Tuesday and had arranged for a conference room at the FBI Office location in Atlanta. He told Jason they would have not only Pierre and Anna

Dupont, but Rowland Davis with them. They wanted to review our notes and speak with all three of them at once to see what one may know that the other may not. Jason told Ronald he would let his office know that he was under the weather and would need to take the remainder of the week off to rest and rejuvenate.

As promised, Special Agents Wilkes and Wright arrived at the FBI office in Atlanta early Tuesday morning and had three other agents with them to escort and ensure the Duponts and Rowland Davis did not attempt to escape. Davis, the Duponts, Wilkes, and Wright entered the conference room reserved by Wilkes. Ronald and Jason were already seated at the large oak-varnished conference table and enjoying a cup of coffee. Wilkes had phoned ahead and asked the front office clerk to allow them to use the conference room until they arrived. The three other agents were posted outside the conference room in the hallway. Wilkes and Wright entered the conference room walking behind Davis and the Duponts. Anna Dupont was crying uncontrollably as she sat down across from Jason and Ronald. Jason stared menacingly at Pierre and Anna. He was pissed with Davis but much more disappointed and angrier with the Duponts.

Pierre broke the silence. "I know you all are angry with my wife and me. That is justified and you're right to be angry. I am sorry for the way we behaved and maybe there were other avenues for us to pursue. We were only thinking about our daughter. Right or wrong."

Jason interrupted him in mid-speech. "You damn right you are sorry you lousy son-of-a-bitch. How many girls have been sold and how many lives ruined by the drugs these people trafficked. You only thought about your daughter and didn't even try to work around these events." Jason had risen from his chair and had begun to circle around the table towards Pierre to confront him or punch his lights out. One of the two or both.

Wilkes stepped in front of Jason and gently pushed him back to his side of the table. "Look guys. Nothing good comes of us trying to correct the past. The Duponts and Mr. Davis will all pay a heavy penalty in money and years for their parts in this entire despicable set of events. All we can do now is try to capture the leader and arrest the members of their syndicate in hopes that no other girls are kidnapped and sold." Jason looked apologetically at Wilkes and angrily sat down in his chair.

"Let's get down to business, "Wright said.

Rowland Davis cleared his throat and began to speak. "I was encountered by a member of the syndicate, and they offered me large sums of money to simply use my warehouse for moving drugs. That is all they told me they were going to move. Not girls. Just drugs. I found out about the girls later. As I said before, they paid me more and more money but eventually threatened my family. When I began to get cold feet, two other members of the syndicate arrived one afternoon after everyone had left for the day, or so I thought and so did they, and carried me into the back of the warehouse. They pointed a gun at my head, cocked the trigger, and asked me if I wanted a .38 caliber slug to pass through my brain. They viciously explained that nothing would change, and I would keep my mouth closed or the last thing I would see before they splattered my brains all over the floor would be the slugs they fired into my wife and kids. I assured them I would remain cooperative and silent. They told me I damn well better or la reine would send me over a few more guests and help me keep my promises and learn how valuable my health insurance was. I am a coward just like the Duponts here." Davis sat slowly back into his chair and hid his face in his hands.

"Wait a second. You said you thought everyone had left for the day. Where was the other person and who were they?" Wright had been making notes meticulously and noticed the earlier information Davis had spoken about.

"I am sorry about that. There was a lazy ass dock worker who had sneaked up into the second-floor loft above the main warehouse floor and fallen asleep while he was hiding from my foreman and his coworkers. The foreman had informed me he was notorious for slipping off unnoticed and not returning for half-hours at the time. We suspected he was sleeping but he always had a plausible story for his whereabouts, and we did not like turnover because it would introduce new people into our workforce, and we did not want anyone to join who might make waves with the operation being run by the syndicate. After the men left, he quickly came down to where I was sitting on a crate of merchandise. I could not move. My knees were knocking so badly, and I was so shaken. I was literally frozen in my footsteps. He asked me if I was ok and did I need him to call the police. I told him no. I knew the dock worker was a Frenchman and asked him if he heard what the man said just before he left. He asked me if I meant the term 'la reine'. I told him I did not speak nor understand very much French. He told me the term meant 'queen', in English."

"That is the same thing Celine told us when we spoke to her last. La reine, the queen. This confirms the fact that we are looking for a woman. What woman and where? IS she in Canada, the US, or handling this operation even more remotely than that?" Wilkes said

"A woman called me once. I sensed she knew Pierre and I were getting cold feet. She was very polite at first. Asking me about my daughter, Louise, and our trip to the park that morning and our picnic brunch there. I asked her how she knew those things and why she was following us. Her tone quickly turned, and she became enraged. She told me to shut the hell up and listen closely. She told me she knew where we lived and our every day-to-day movement and if I didn't want my daughter to have an accident, I best encourage Pierre to continue to assist her business operations as usual," Anna said. Still crying.

"Did you recognize the voice? What was the number? Do you think you could recognize the voice if you heard it again?" Ronald was hoping Anna may be able to identify the lady or provide a number?

"The number was a burner cell phone. This lady was a pro. Pierre had one of his contacts with the RCMP special operations run a check to see what cell tower the number pinged from last. He told Pierre that it would show a location in Beijing for a couple of seconds, then Moscow, then Bogota, and then several other international locations during the call. These people are well funded and very skilled at what they do. Could I recognize the voice, if I heard it again? I could never forget the icy tones and sheer venom of that voice. She also told me that no one crosses la reine. NO ONE! "

"It sounds like this lady is very proud of her moniker and very dangerous. I need the three of you to list every lady you had contact with concerning what may have been trafficking related and even normal business operations. I understand this will take some time. I will work with Pierre and Anna. Jeff, can you work with Rowland? We can take a couple of weeks compiling the list of names and see if any of them cross-reference or you all decide may make a more viable person of interest and we can begin with them. I am not letting this drop and awaiting another kidnapped person. This lady does not make mistakes, and we are going to need to make our own breaks in the case. Ronald and Jason, if you two think of anything and I mean anything that may assist, please call me immediately. The further we go down this rabbit hole and the more we learn about this demon, really starts to piss me off more and more. We will need to touch base with Sheriff Powers and arrange to use his prison facilities to house Davis and the Duponts. I can arrange that myself and will speak with him right after our meeting. Ronald, could you assist Jeff with the transport of the three of them and I will stay in touch after that and keep you posted on any new developments," Madison said. Visibly angry and more determined than ever to drive this case to resolution.

Jeff and Ronald handcuffed Davis and the Duponts and led them away to their respective cruisers for transport to the Fulton County Prison. Madison had made the call to Powers right after they left, and he readily agreed to assist with housing the prisoners and handling anything related to the case. Powers was still upset with himself on the way he had handled the situation with Brice Staley and desperately wanted to make amends for the error in judgement of that fatal afternoon. Jason returned home and would call the office and arrange for a loading the next morning. He would be ready when called upon but needed to get back on the road and generate some salary for his family.

Chapter 17

Ronald's Discovery

Days went about normally for Ronald and Jason the next couple of weeks. Ronald was in Glynn County keeping its citizens safe. Jason and Lindsey were preparing April and Lauren for the fourth grade and first grade. Autumn had arrived and the girls were excited about seeing their friends each day and Lindsey was a tad bit ready for them to be there. She loved them with her whole heart, but she had handled them both the entire summer practically by herself as Jason had been assisting Ronald and Special Agents Wright and Wilkes. Lindsey had decided she may go back to school and pursue her early education degree and perhaps enter the teaching field. She was home a lot with both girls in school and Jason on the road. She wanted to help shape young children's foundational learning years and the extra income would be beneficial when the girls were ready for college. Jason supported her one hundred percent and was even more excited that she could do a bulk of the work online. Jason would never forget the horror of what happened to him due to la reine but he was becoming more and more of himself with Lindsey's love and support and father time. He looked forward to the updates Wilkes would pass along to Ronald and then in-kind Ronald would pass along to Jason.

According to Wilkes, the names being provided by Davis and the Duponts did not produce any concrete leads. It appeared la reine was utilizing a number of different people within her syndicate to carry out the illegal activities. Wilkes had asked Jeff Wright to question the Duponts separately as she questioned Davis in hopes that one person would not influence another unintentionally. Wilkes informed Ronald that she had no intentions on stepping down the speed and efforts of the pursuit but may need to recalibrate and regroup on another plan of attack. Ronald assured her he knew she had the investigation's best interest in mind and would proceed as needed and he would support it accordingly.

Ronald was a little bummed about the lack of traction the discussions with Davis and the Duponts had generated but he remained the eternal optimist. Wilkes and Wright were about to transport the three of them back to their respective prisons in the next two days. Ronald had reached for the cell phone on his desk to call Jason and let him know that the question of Davis and the Duponts had fizzled, and it was necessary for Wilkes and Wright to pursue other avenues when an incoming call popped in. He saw the call was from Wright and not Wilkes. Ronald answered the call, and it was indeed Jeff Wright on the other end of the call.

"What do I owe this special occasion? You never call me. It is generally Madison providing the updates."

"Well, I wish I could say it was with great news and the syndicate leader had been identified and arrested. I even wish I could say it was good news and let you know that we had a hot new lead. However, I am in a little bit of trouble. I scanned over to your email at the Sheriff's Office the lists Madison and I compiled from our discussions Davis and the Duponts. When Madison found out she hit the ceiling. She did not want those passed along until we had an opportunity to cross-reference those further. She wanted to review my list and hers and have me do the same. I was not sure why she was so upset but she is the senior agent on the assignment, and I am calling you to instruct you to delete the email and remove it permanently from your trash. We will send over the revised and final version once we have discussed things as a twosome. Please do this immediately Ronald and I appreciate your help." Wright had a note of concern in his voice, and it was obvious Madison had ripped him a new one for what she must have felt was a major oversight.

"Of course. I will handle it right away. I appreciate the call, and I will send a text message to confirm completion of the request when I have completed," Ronald was reassuring in his voice as he ended the call.

As soon as he had ended the call with Jeff Wright, his phone was buzzing again. He looked down at the screen and saw Madison's name and number appear. He pushed away from his desk and computer as he was about to delete the email Jeff had scanned over. He leaned back in his chair and answered the call.

"Did Agent Wright call you?" Madison did not make an effort to greet Ronald and was very agitated.

"Yes, he did. He explained to me he had scanned over some documents before discussing with you and asked that I delete the email and remove it from my trash folder. I was in the process of handling that when your call came in. He and I had not hung up on the call for more than fifteen seconds when your call came in."

"Please do. I am sorry for being so direct. I cannot believe he did that without consulting with me first. He has no comprehension of the chain of command. How is your day? I was hoping we would find a solid lead in those names but as of now nothing is jumping out at me," Madison's said.

"All good here and no worries. Just keep hammering away on the case and let us know if we can assist. I hope to hear from you soon."

Agent Wright was anxious as he had already texted Ronald and asked him if the request he made had been completed. Ronald texted back saying he had been momentarily distracted but was handling now. Jeff told him that it was not necessary to respond as he knew he would handle it. Ronald set the phone down once more, pulled the chair back under his desk, and reached for the mouse to delete the email. As he hovered over the email and was about to click delete, he suddenly stopped and rocked back in his desk chair. He stared at the ceiling for what felt like hours but was only a few seconds. Ronald had always followed his gut as a lawman and his gut was telling him something just wasn't adding up. He was not sure what it was, but something was gnawing at him about the email and how quickly Madison had reached out right after the call from Jeff. Ronald was an honest man and had never gone back on his word as an officer, but this was troubling him. He clicked open on the email and clicked on the PDF file. The two separate lists of names were within the PDF and Ronald printed them off.

Ronald stepped over to the printer and collected the two pages of paperwork. He walked back over to his desk, eyeing the list as he walked. He slowly sat down in his desk chair never taking his eyes off the paperwork. He placed the papers down on his desk side-by-side and shifted his look from one page to the other. He picked up a pencil which was lying beside a picture of his girlfriend and began to circle something on each one of the pages. He looked up and shook his head. He quickly reached for his cell phone and called Jason.

Jason answered on the second ring. "What the hell do you want? I am busy trying to make a living while you are taking your girlfriend to the beach for a three-day weekend and drinking beer."

"Hey buddy. I can't explain right now, but how close to home are you? I need to come see you right away. It is important," Ronald had been oblivious to what Jason had said and was drilled in closely on what he had circled on the paperwork.

"I had a run to Birmingham today and I am about two hours from home. I can probably beat you there and will wait for you to arrive. If I get jammed up in Atlanta traffic, Lindsey is home, and she can hang out with you until I arrive. What the hell is up man?"

"I don't want to explain over the phone. I am leaving now and will be there in three hours. I will be lights flashing as I travel so I do not get hung up in traffic."

Ronald hung up the phone without saying goodbye and scooped up the two pages of paperwork. He walked quickly out of his office and mumbled to the front desk clerk that he would be back tomorrow. As promised, he immediately turned on the lights and raced out of the parking lot of the Sheriff's Office. He arrived at Jason's house three hours later and saw Jason's rig across the street in its usual parking spot in the empty lot. He jumped out of his cruiser, clutching the two pieces of paperwork in his right hand. He rang the doorbell and walked in small, anxious circles as he awaited someone to answer the door.

"Hey Uncle Ronald. Mama and Daddy are in the living room," Lauren said. Her two front teeth were missing from her smile.

Ronald picked up Lauren and carried her into the living room where Lindsey and Jason were sitting on the loveseat. Ronald set Lauren down gently, kissed her on the cheek, grabbed a nearby chair, and pulled it up to Jason at the loveseat. He managed to greet the two of them before he began to unfold the paperwork and speak.

"Ok, you guys hear me out. This is going to sound farfetched and way out of left field but when my daddy was Sheriff, he led with his gut and so have I. My gut tells me something is not quite right here. I need someone to confirm my feelings or tell me I am completely crazy."

"It may be farfetched, but I know you are a damn good officer of the law, and I believe in your hunches. Tell us about it and let's see what's up."

"Ok. So, I received a call from Jeff Wright asking me to delete and permanently remove the paperwork he just scanned over to my email account. I told him I would and was about to delete it when no sooner than I hung up with Jeff, Madison was calling me. She was all pissed off at Jeff and she asked me to delete the same file. I was about to delete it when she and I hung up, but something told me not to do it. I have never disobeyed a request from a fellow law officer, but I just could not get this nagging feeling to go away. I printed off the paperwork and began to look at the names Jeff and Madison had listed down from their separate discussions with Rowland Davis and the Duponts. I began to find several names that each interview had garnished. These names circled were mentioned in both interviews."

"Ok. I see where both interviews had similar names. What is the significance of that? I am sure Wilkes and Wright will pursue these people and question them," Jason said.

"I spoke with Wilkes, and she told me they were getting ready to transport Davis and the Duponts back to their respective prisons. She also told me there were no concrete leads in the names she and Wright put together. Why would she say that? There are at least three names here that are on both lists. She would not have to give me specifics, but she could have and quite honestly should have told me there were matches. It would be fine if they wanted to run the investigation into each of the names and ask us to help where needed. Why the deception? Why the sudden rush to have Wright call me and ask me to delete the information? Why did she call so quickly afterwards? Is it that big of a deal that I had a copy of the list as much as we have assisted on this? Why was she so angry at Wright? I know this is not cool, but what does she have to hide and who better to derail an investigation than someone leading it. Do you see where I am going with this?"

"I see where you are going and man this looks like a bad, bad road. Do you really think she may be involved? Worst yet. Do you think she is la reine? Was the leader of the syndicate in the same rooms as we were and asking questions of people she had assisted in apprehending? What do we do now? Where do we go to check this out? Who else could be involved at her level? This is spooky," Jason said with a grimace.

"I hate to do this, but I have a friend with the GBI that has access for federal level background checks and information. I trust her and I am going to reach out to her and see what she may be able to uncover and provide for us. Her name is Lydia Stringfellow and she helped me on a case several years ago. She is a tough officer with the GBI and will do all she can for us."

Ronald stepped outside to call Lydia and Jason and Lindsey sat in silence staring at paperwork Ronald had shown them and was trying to process the information. Ronald was outside for fifteen minutes or so and then stepped back into the house. He walked over to the loveseat where Jason and Lindsey were still sitting in silence and told them Lydia was working on the information he requested but it would take a couple of days. Lydia trusted Ronald explicitly but she could not hand over certain information to Ronald as it was proprietary. If there was anything unusual that flagged on Madison's check, she would pass it along, but Lydia's office would have to become involved moving forward. Ronald decided to return to Brunswick and handle his office duties there and await word from Lydia. Jason would return to work, and he would await further word from Ronald.

Could Madison be the leader? Finally, the road may be coming to an end but what a sad ending it would be if it turns out to be true. Lindsey, Jason, and Ronald never shared this thought with each other, but all seemed to be thinking the same thing.

CHAPTER 18

This Cannot Be True

Jason was pulling away from the warehouse in Birmingham. This seemed to be his newly assigned route, and he was enjoying it. His family liked it, too. He was making a decent wage running that route and he was home almost every evening barring an issue at the warehouse location there. The ladies in his life enjoyed seeing him each night. He loved being there, also. It had been three days and no word from Lydia. Ronald would text Jason each day and let him know that there were no new developments. Jason, in his heart, hoped Ronald was wrong, but in his mind, he feared the worst. He would have to wait for the news. Jason had to swing by the office at Staley's to check on some back pay Mrs. Rube had messaged him about. He wasn't sure what it could be for, but Mrs. Rube was showing herself to be very fair and generous to her associates. Besides, Jason was not about to turn down any money. He could spoil his girls with the extra cash. He pulled up into the truck parking area at Staley's right after 5:00 p.m.. The associate parking lot was empty with of course one exception, Kelly was there still working. Jason surprised but Rube's car was gone also. He knew Kelly would be able to help him, so he made his way towards the main office building and up the steps.

"Well, hello, sunshine. How's the most important person at Staley's doing today?"

"I'm ok. Just not too sure about the 'most important person here' part. Mrs. Rube may have something to say about that," Kelly said with a bright smile.

Kelly knew her desk and her appearance was the first thing visitors saw, and she wanted to make a good impression. She would clean the pen and pencil caddy, her business card holder, the picture frame housing a photo of her and her doggie, her desk and desk chair was immaculate, and even down to her name plate and holder. She put her best foot forward.

"Mrs. Rube messaged me about some pay issue, and I wanted to see if you knew what it was pertaining to. I am sure you know all about it as you are always on top of everything. I do not know how you accomplish everything. I hope you know how much everyone appreciates you."

Kelly began blushing. "You are too sweet, Jason. I love my job, coworkers, and customers. It makes me happy. Actually, Mrs. Rube wanted you to get the quarterly bonus she implemented after she bought the business. She has been great for the associates and morale here, hasn't she?"

Kelly smiled and handed the check to Jason.

"I feel bad about accepting a bonus. I was barely here last quarter. I better not turn it down because Mrs. Rube will be insulted and Lindsey will be angry if she knew I turned down her mani-pedi money," Jason said with a laugh.

"How is the investigation going? Are they close to finding the horrible person behind all of that evilness? I hope they do soon. Also, tell Lindsey to enjoy the mani-pedi."

"I will let her know. By the way, you missed a spot on your nameplate. You need to get some brass polish and shine it up."

Jason was driving home in his pickup. He left his rig at Staley's because he would be taking tomorrow as rest to reset his DOT downtime requirement. He had the windows down in the pickup as it was an abnormally cool afternoon for this time of year. He had the radio blasting the best of the 1980's and his hair was blowing in the wind as he sang along to every song that was played. Suddenly, he stopped singing, turned down the radio, and pulled over. He fumbled furiously for his cell phone which was resting in the seat beside him. He was shaking so badly he could barely hold the phone steady as he looked for Ronald's contact in his address book. He stopped shaking long enough to hit call on Ronald's number and awaited his answer.

"You have got to get your ass up here immediately. I think I have stumbled onto something. Have you heard anything from your friend Lydia? I think we are closer to this than we think. I don't want to explain it over the phone. Can you leave first thing in the morning? I'm off tomorrow. We need to check with your friend Lydia and get Wright down here with the Duponts as soon as he can. I know this is short notice, but make it happen, please," Jason said with a crack in his voice.

"Ok. I will be there first thing in the morning. I will see if Wright can swing a trip by himself and make Madison think we just wanted to speak to the Duponts once more to cover some questions about their daughters. It is a long shot, and he will have to be creative, but I think he can pull it off."

Ronald was sitting in Jason's driveway the next morning at 7:00 a.m.. He had left Brunswick very early to beat any rush hour heading into Atlanta. Jason heard the car pull into the driveway and was standing with the door open as Ronald walked up the drive. He let his friend inside and closed the door behind them. The two men sat down at the kitchen table and Jason poured them a cup of coffee. Lindsey left around 6:30 a.m. taking the girls to school. The men had the house to themselves.

"Good morning. You sounded like you had seen a ghost yesterday man. What the hell is going on, Jason?"

"I was riding along the freeway yesterday with the windows down and radio blasting. It helps me think."

"What does that God awful singing help you do?" Ronald asked.

"I have the voice of an angel. Back to my story. The music was cranking, wind blowing, and I was thinking about this whole idea that Madison was tied into this somehow. I just did not want to believe it. However, when she wanted to question Davis and not the Duponts, it got me thinking. Then it hit me like a ton of bricks. Did you speak with your GBI friend and Jeff Wright? I do not want to get too far ahead of myself.

"Yes. I spoke with Lydia. What does Madison not wanting to question the Duponts have to do with her potentially being involved in all of this?

You remember when you asked Anna Dupont if she could recognize the voice of the lady who called her that day and threatened Louise? Anna Dupont was crying so uncontrollably and sobbing so badly she probably couldn't have recognized anyone's voice that day. I was thinking if Madison questioned a much calmer Anna Dupont in a less stressful environment than the day we were there, she might recognize Madison's voice during the questioning. Besides, why wouldn't Wright and Madison question both sets of folks?"

Jason was about to go on when Ronald interrupted. "One second. I see your logic, but I spoke with Lydia, and she is more connected than I ever imagined. She spoke with one of the top officials in Madison's department and they confirmed exactly what the deep dive background check Lydia performed. There has never been a more honorable agent on the team than Madison Wilkes. Lydia said this guy kept going on and raving about her dedication and honesty. Lydia said she went back to preschool on the lady, and she has never been to a visit to the principal's office let alone any criminal acts."

"The fact that she checks out makes me feel so relieved. I am glad she is one of the good guys. Where does that lead us next? I have an idea, but I need Anna Dupont and Madison here. I would still like Anna to hear Madison's voice over the telephone. Let me fill you in."

"Do you think it is someone on the list we looked at?" Ronald asked.

"It just may be, but I want to make sure."

The two men sat and talked for another hour as Jason laid out his theory and Ronald processed what Jason was saying. He could not believe what Jason was suggesting at first but as he continued to listen, it made more and more sense. Ronald called Jeff Wright and asked if he could get Anna Dupont and Madison to Atlanta. Wright explained that he tried everything, and Wilkes wasn't buying any of it. She had no issue with Anna coming to Atlanta, but she insisted on traveling with them. Jason called a friend of his who owned a rival trucking company in Atlanta and asked if they could use one of his offices the day after tomorrow. It would be Friday and that would work perfectly according to what Jason wanted to attempt to do. The friend had no issue with him using the office and the plan was now in place. Ronald would stay the next two evenings at Jason's home, and they would put the plan into action first thing Friday morning. By that time, Wilkes and Wright would have Anna Dupont back in the facility Sheriff Powers had previously provided and they could arrange for her to be at the friend's office, also.

Friday morning arrived and everyone arrived at Tight Man's Trucking. Wilkes and Wright emerged from a loaner Sheriff's cruiser courtesy of Sheriff Powers, and they had Anna Dupont along with them. Joshua showed them into one of his conference rooms at the rear of the main building so they could have complete silence.

"Agent Wilkes, could you ask Joshua for a landline telephone, please?" Ronald asked.

He was already seated, and Wilkes was near the door. She stepped out and headed down the corridor to retrieve a landline telephone.

As she reached the front of the complex, she heard her cell phone ring. "Hello? Hello? I cannot hear you. You need to return the call when you are in a better area." She retrieved the phone and headed back down the corridor toward the conference room. The people inside were able to hear her as she attempted to answer the call and now heard her walking back toward the room. Ronald looked over at Anna Dupont and she shook her head negatively.

Once back inside the conference room. Madison took a seat at the large conference room table and Ronald plugged the landline telephone into a phone jack near the table. He looked closely at Anna Dupont and gave her careful instructions on how to handle the call she was about to be asked to place. He instructed her not to speak very frequently because if this was the person who she spoke with the day her daughter was threatened, she did not want to give away the fact that it was her. Also, they needed the person who answered to speak more often to ensure a positive identification could be made. Ronald instructed everyone to be completely silent once the number was dialed. The phone call would be recorded and played back for everyone once Anna had made the identification.

Anna dialed the number for a business Ronald had written down on a slip of paper in front of her. She was visibly shaken but holding herself very well, considering the circumstances. The line rang twice, and a lady answered. Anna asked if she could speak to Mr. Morgan Troy. The voice on the other end of the line sounded confused and responded that there was no Morgan Troy at this number. Just as the lady was about to hang up, Anna blurted out and apologized. She corrected herself and asked if the person could provide the address she was located at as she had heard from a friend that this was a solid referral. The lady on the other end of the phone provided the address and asked who the referral was. Anna informed her it was Morgan Troy, and she had been a little ahead of herself when she first spoke. She asked the lady her name and if she could tell her who the best point of contact would be when she arrived and how late they would be there. The lady revealed her name, began to rattle off several names as a point of contact in the sales department, and said they were open for business Monday to Friday and held normal business hours. Anna began to turn pale as the lady spoke. Ronald could see she was becoming disoriented and motioned with his hands to wrap up the call. Anna could barely get out a response of thanks and hung up quickly. She missed the cradle with the telephone receiver and Jason hurriedly picked up the receiver and placed it in the cradle to ensure the person on the other end of the line did not hear or suspect anything. Anna sank back into her chair, buried her head in her hands, and began to wail rivers of tears. Jason leaned in to console her and she quickly turned away. The group allowed her to regain her composure for several minutes.

Finally, Madison spoke. "Mrs. Dupont, can we assume this was the person who called you that day and threatened your daughter?"

"Yes. That was the devil that threatened my Louise. Her voice immediately chilled my bones and brought back the sick feeling I felt that day. Undeniably, that bitch is the sick, depraved soul you are seeking. I would stake my Louise's life on it," Anna buried her head in her hands again and tears rolled between her shaking hands and down both sides of her cheeks.

Ronald shot a glance over at Jason, who shot an even more astonishing glance back. The color had left Jason's face and Ronald starred in utter amazement. The silence was deafening as no one in the room was in on the secret that Jason and Ronald shared. Each person sat quietly in their chairs for what felt like hours but was only a few seconds.

"Ok guys, let us in on what you two have theorized and apparently Mrs. Dupont has confirmed. We need to move swiftly here and bring this person in for questioning," Agent Wright said.

"Please meet us at this address at 5:30 p.m. and bring enough people to surround the home location." Ronald had now jotted down the address and passed it to Wright and Wilkes.

"With all due respect Sheriff Watts, we aren't going anywhere until you tell us why and everything you two gentlemen have uncovered and have postulated. I respect leads and other law enforcement officers, but I am not firing off and mobilizing a tactical arrest team until I know the specifics. All the specifics," Wilkes said, leaning forward in her chair with a stern look upon her face.

Jason inched forward into his chair and began to speak to the group. He laid out his theory on who he thought it was and why he thought it was. He thought back to the paperwork he had on his load to Laredo and how the CTPAT serial number had been modified. How could someone notice this so easily after he had spent hours looking over it? This thought turned to other thoughts. Then the light came on. He knew. Jason stated that he wished he was wrong and sometimes quite honestly wished he never thought of this lady's connection. Jason explained how it pained him to even think that someone he cared about, loved even, could do something like this. He had to know. He explained that he had called Ronald and told him everything he knew and some things he suspected. Mrs. Dupont had now confirmed what he had feared.

"I'll be damned. It was right there in front of you all this time. Jason, I am so sorry. I will mobilize a team to the home address and take care of this," Wilkes was dialing up agent support from the Fulton County area before she finished speaking.

Ronald reached out and hugged his friend. Wright had called in one of the agents to have Anna Dupont transported to the prison Sheriff Powers had arranged for her to be kept at and explained that they would transport her back to her assigned prison after this mission was closed out. Wilkes, Wright, Ronald, and Jason headed for the door at Tight Man's Trucking to drive to the location provided by Ronald and Jason. It was now 4:45 p.m.. The drive would take about fifteen minutes and allow everyone to get into place before these four people moved in for the arrest. Jason had been sworn in again as Ronald's temporary deputy to make Jason's entrance legal, viable, and if injured, to ensure a civilian was not reported among the wounded.

CHAPTER 19

The Mystery Unravels
and Answers Abound

Ronald and Jason arrived at the same time as Wright and Wilkes. The four of them looked at their cell phones and saw it was 5:25 p.m.. They had waited at the end of the road to allow the tactical team to get into place and ensure there were no possible slip ups and any avenues of escape. They walked swiftly to the door and entered with Jason taking the lead.

"Hey there sweetheart. What brings you here so early? Where is your truck? I don't see it outside."

"Please be quiet. These people have some questions to ask you, and it would be in your best interest to answer them honestly and in-depth," Jason said.

"I know Ronald. Who are these other people? Why are they here? Are you mad at me, sweetheart?"

"Do not call me that. You lost the right to say that when I figured out just what a sick person I've known all these years."

Wilkes spoke up. "Ms. Kelly Parton, we are here to question you about your involvement in human trafficking and drugs. You have the right to remain silent and the right to an attorney. Do you understand these rights?"

"What the hell are they talking about Jason? I am not involved in anything illegal."

"Please direct your answers to me or Special Agent Wright. My name is Special Agent Madison Wilkes. We have been advised of information that links you to a human trafficking and drug operation that was discovered in Windsor, Canada and traced back to Brice Staley here at Staley's Trucking."

Kelly had begun to cry. "Yes. I know about that, and Brice and Quinn are dead. They were the ones behind it all."

"We have further information from some of the victims and a voice recognition from a person you threatened during the commission of these crimes. We need you to accompany us to FBI headquarters here in Atlanta and obtain a full statement," Wilkes moved forward to handcuff Kelly, and she pulled away.

"Wait a damn minute. You have the wrong person," Kelly shouted.

"Too many facts point to you," Jason said. "You were privy to all the manifests, you knew Brice had that manual typewriter in his cabinet, you used it to alter the CTPAT serial number on my paperwork, you worked with Quinn to ensure he was the Windsor driver once you bought him off. You used Brice and threatened his family, the same way you threatened the Duponts. We were getting close, and you crashed Quinn's computer in his rig. You have master access to the software system in each of the trucks. I am sure Brice granted and installed that after he was in too deep. The software issue made all fingers point to Quinn. Quinn was dead and now the syndicate leader and his operation are a thing of the past. However, you couldn't stop. I am not sure if it was your greed, power trip, or just pure evil, but you couldn't stop. The girl you had kidnapped was found and rescued in Denver. You asked me about booking a flight for Ronald and me to Denver. You never booked a flight for anyone in this office before. It was one of the few things you never did. I slipped up and told you we were going to Quebec. You knew we would speak with the Duponts. We were getting closer and didn't even realize it. I guess you decided to let things cool off some or you became extra cautious as other girls and drugs were not located having the same pattern as your operation. I will be honest; I had just about given up hope of ever locating the syndicate boss until I stopped by here to check on the bonus payment Mrs. Rube was providing everyone here at Staley's Trucking. You were pleasant, as always, and cleaning your area, as you so often do. It had never hit me before and didn't hit me that day until I had driven almost all the way home. Your mahogany name holder and golden name plate. You had cleaned it to a shine and polished the golden plate. Then it dawned on me what those French girls and others were hearing, la reine, the queen. The damn queen," Jason was shouting as he spoke more and more and pointing angrily at the golden name plate on Kelly's desk.

Kelly's incessant sobbing suddenly stopped. "You're so damn smart but you don't know everything. I am the QUEEN and will always be the QUEEN, but I can't do it alone.

"We are sure you have an elaborate network of associates in your syndicate, but you are about to name names, and we are going to shut them down," Agent Wright said.

"You want names. I will give you some damn names and I will start with the most important member of my organization," Kelly stammered as she spoke and sobbed.

"Get her ass out of here. I don't want anything to fall through the cracks here. She needs to have an attorney present, and we want this to be an ironclad arrest and conviction," Agent Wilkes said as she walked toward Kelly with handcuffs taken out of her gun belt.

Kelly pushed away from Wilkes and took several steps toward Ronald as if to shield herself. Ronald grabbed her by both arms and began to slowly walk towards Madison so she could slap the handcuffs on Kelly. She pulled away furiously and backed up against the wall. Staring directly at Madison. She would not take her eyes off her.

"NO! NO! I will not go with this bitch anywhere. She will kill me. You want to know who my top operative is? You have been working alongside her for this entire investigation. Special

Agent Madison Wilkes. She is bought and paid for by me. I needed someone in the bureau to keep me posted on movements, checkpoint areas, and where the most advantageous points were to move these girls and our drugs. Her hands are dirty, and I can prove it. You can arrest me, and I will go willingly, but not with her. Once we are at FBI headquarters here in Atlanta, I will lay it all out for you. "

"She is trying to talk her way into a plea deal. I have been trying to apprehend her and her group along with all of you. I am not a master criminal. I have spent my career serving justice. Besides, Ronald, you had your friend run a check on me. Did it turn up anything? I can answer that, it did not. Why didn't it show any illegal activity, money, indiscretions? Because there is nothing to find. She is going to FBI headquarters, and she can go with any of you. I don't care as long as she goes to jail for a very long time. That is all I am interested in."

Ronald stared at Madison in amazement. "How did you…? Did Lydia? I am sorry Agent Wilkes. We were just checking every angle and….. I had no right. Please accept my apology."

"Don't apologize. You did what a good investigator and law enforcement officer does. You check all the boxes and eliminate people one by one. However, you don't get to the position I am in without knowing a few people, making friends, and having contacts in special places. When your friend Lydia ran my background and did her investigation, she asked an old friend of mine who works with her at the GBI and he reported back to me that she was looking into my history. All is well and I have nothing, and I mean nothing to hide. "

Agent Wright had handcuffed Kelly and reminded her and encouraged her to exercise her right to be silent. Kelly had stopped talking and simply said she would lay everything out when they arrived at headquarters and her attorney arrived. Everyone began to make their way out of the building when Jason tugged at Ronald's shirt sleeve and pointed to Kelly's purse and briefcase behind her desk. Ronald called out to Wright and Wilkes and let them know to go ahead and they would gather up Kelly's belongings and her laptop. They were sure there would be syndicate information encrypted on there and would further implicate her and identify people in the organization. As Jason and Ronald looked up as the front door of the office clanged shut, they began to box up all the contents on Kelly's desk and her personal effects, and laptop.

As soon as they exited the building they were stopped dead in their tracks by a loud pop. Agent Wright had stepped to the rear of the cruiser to open the rear door so he could place Kelly inside. When he stepped away from her to open the door, a shot rang out. Kelly was shot in the back and the bullet exited her heart killing her instantly.

Ronald ran up to Wilkes and Wright beside the cruiser and Kelly's lifeless body. Jason was still standing at the top of the stairs looking out in amazement and disbelief. The other agents who had been positioned around the property were now racing up on foot and in cruisers with sirens and lights blaring. Ronald reached down and checked for a pulse on Kelly's neck, but it was no use. Kelly Parton, the syndicate queen, was dead.

"She tried to run. When Jeff went to open the rear door, Ms. Parton looked back at me and saw there was distance between us, and she tried to run. I was aiming for her arm to wound her and make her fall to the ground. When she turned to run, her back flashed toward me and the shot went into her back. The objective was to wound her," Agent Wilkes was shaking and having difficulty speaking.

Madison leaned against the car and placed her revolver back into her holster. One of the agents made a call to 911 for an ambulance and the coroner. Jason looked at Ronald and asked if he was needed any longer. Ronald told him no and he would catch up with him later tonight. Jason slowly walked to the end of the drive leading up to the building looking down at Kelly as he passed by. He had requested a UBER on his cell phone and would be home shortly. The agents and Ronald would need to stay behind and prepare statements and reports to close out the case.

Ronald arrived at Jason's home around 10:00 p.m.. Lindsey and Jason had sat at the kitchen table and talked about the case, Kelly's involvement, and her death since the time Jason arrived home. Ronald tapped on the front door lightly, as he did not want to wake the girls up and let himself in. He walked into the kitchen, hugged Lindsey, and sat down at the table with them. Lindsey stood up and stepped over to the counter to get Ronald a cup of coffee and to refill her and Jason's cups, also.

"You know Jason. Something did not sit well with me. I believe Kelly was the mastermind of the syndicate and although I am sorry she was killed, I feel she received a fate better than she deserved. I cannot shake the idea that she was killed to ensure her silence. I cannot get the idea that what she was saying about Madison Wilkes is true. I know that sounds crazy and I should not think that about a fellow law enforcement officer, but I cannot get it out of my head that she is somehow involved in all the syndicate's activities. I had my friend Lydia meet me at Sheriff Powers' office after we left the crime scene and I took Kelly's laptop with me. I asked her not to tell anyone where she was going or what it was pertaining to. When she arrived, we worked with the IT team at the Sheriff's Office. We saw a number of dates, names, phone numbers, addresses, bank accounts, and trafficking information on the laptop. There was one name that came up repeatedly."

"Please do not tell me the name is Madison Wilkes," Jason interrupted.

"No. it was not Madison Wilkes. While I was reviewing the information in the laptop further. Lydia was running the names found on the laptop through her background software. We wanted to get a list of these people out to the FBI as soon as possible tomorrow morning and start having them arrested and brought in for questioning. We saw the Duponts, Rowland Davis, Quinn Brown, and many others. All the names brought back information and with one exception. A lady named Roxanne Windermere. There wasn't any information on the lady anywhere. Lydia did extensive searches for nearly an hour and the name would not return anything. I was about to chalk it up to this person not having anything to do with Kelly's syndicate and just tell Lydia to forget about it, then it dawned on me. I had seen that name somewhere. It took me a few minutes of deep thought and recollection, but I finally realized where I had seen it. Roxanne Windermere was on the list of names the Duponts and Davis compiled when Agents Wilkes and Wright interviewed them."

"Yes. I remember that. You said Wright was calling you and was upset because Wilkes had chewed his ass about sending over confidential information or something like that," Jason said.

"Exactly. If you remember, Madison called me right after Wright called even before I could click delete on the file. I recall Roxanne Windermere's name was on both lists. Rowland Davis listed her and the Duponts, also."

"So, who is this Roxanne person and how does she fit into the syndicate?" Lindsey asked. Now she too was engrossed in what Ronald was postulating.

"I am not sure. I have Lydia checking on her for me further. Do you think I could grab a shower and sleep here tonight? I want to meet Lydia first thing tomorrow morning and see what she has come up with. "

"Of course. Let me go put fresh linens on the guest bed and get you a towel and washcloth for the shower."

"What do you really think is going on with this Roxanne Windermere lady, Ronald?"

"Man, I do not know, but it is driving me nuts. I want to get everyone on Kelly's list and damn it, I just want to know who this person is. My gut says she is larger in this operation than any of us can imagine."
"As Scarlett O'Hara said in *Gone with the Wind,* tomorrow is another day. Let's get some rest and get an early, fresh start in the morning. It has been a helluva long day. "

CHAPTER 20

Roxanne

The next morning Ronald and Jason met in the kitchen where Lindsey was already making breakfast and brewing some coffee. Just as they sat down to eat, Ronald's cell phone buzzed with a text from Lydia asking him to call her. Ronald dialed the number and put her on speaker. She answered on the first ring.

"Good morning, young lady. How are you? Hope you have some news for us. By the way, I have you on speaker and Jason and his wife are in the room.

"I wanted to call you first thing. I know you were anxious about information on Roxanne Windermere and how she fit into all of this. I have some semi-good news and some not good news at all. Please pull the video up I just sent and stay on the call with me, please. "

Ronald pulled up the video and let Lydia know he was playing it. "It looks like a lady walking across a tarmac to a private jet. Where is this? Is this the Atlanta Airport?"

"It is the Atlanta airport, and it was 7:30 PM last night. I was able to get more information on Roxanne from Kelly's laptop. It seems Kelly was the leader but had a very important and connected second in command. She had an entire file encrypted on her laptop dedicated to Roxanne Windermere. If you are done viewing the first video I sent, please pull up the second video I just sent now."

Ronald pulled up the video and he and Jason stopped breathing. The person walking across the tarmac toward the aircraft was Special Agent Madison Wilkes.

Roxanne Windermere is Madison Wilkes. Kelly had everything Madison had assisted on during the drug and human trafficking. It is over fifty pages long. These ladies had been at this a long time. I guess Kelly was not going to go down alone, if things went south. When I began to cross-reference activity between Madison Wilkes and Roxanne, bank accounts surfaced, passports under both names popped up, and international underground contact names and numbers surfaced. Kelly was damn good at this operation gentlemen, but Madison is a professional. No, she is a Rembrandt in a world of amateur artists."

"I assume you can trace the aircraft serial number she was on and its destination. Let's get in touch with the police in that area and have her picked up and extradited back to the United States," Ronald was optimistic they could catch Madison and bring her to justice.

"I traced the aircraft and flight information. There is nothing we can do. We can't even lock down her accounts as the funds were transferred last night to a bank in the Caymans and they will not cooperate and cannot be forced to cooperate," Lydia said.

"What in the hell do you mean? There is nothing we can do?" Jason was growing angry and was almost shouting into the phone.

"The flight destination was the Maldives. The Gulfstream Jet is owned by one of the people listed in Kelly's database which means he owns the plane and will not have it turned around. It will land in the Maldives. We can add hindering prosecution to his charges when we pick him up, but there is no way to stop the flight. It only has a few more hours and would not have enough fuel to detour off course, even if he would cooperate. "

'Ok! Have someone at the airport in the Maldives and take her into custody there."

"We can't," whispered Ronald defeatedly.

"What?"

"There is no extradition treaty between the Maldives and the United States," Ronald spoke up a little louder this time and exhaled deeply.

"I am sorry, Ronald. I just wanted you to know. I wish I had better news. Madison Wilkes/Roxanne Windermere is gone." Lydia was apologetic as she ended the call.

Ronald looked up at Jason and then over at Lindsey. No one could speak. They stared at each other for a few seconds in complete shock.

Jason slammed a fist against the table. "No," he yelled. "We can't let her win. There must be a way to get justice for everyone who was hurt because of her."

For now, there's not a single thing we can do," Ronald said.

"Maybe we can come with a way to trick her into going somewhere else. Somewhere that does have an extradition treaty with the United States. "

Ronald stared at Jason for several seconds. A series of emotions crossed over his face. Disappointment, doubt, defeat, and then, realization and hope. Jason perked up in his seat waiting for Ronald to have just an ounce of good news. Finally, Ronald gave a small smile and opened his mouth.

"I might have an idea."

CHAPTER 21

Is This the End?

The days turned into weeks. Ronald had not mentioned anything to Jason or Lydia about Madison. He would call and text them and see how they and their loved ones were doing but nothing in the way of updates on his undisclosed plan about capturing and having Madison extradited to the United States. Jason did not initially ask Ronald about his plans or how the operation was progressing, but he grew more curious and, quite honestly, restless about the fact that Ronald either had no viable plan or was not allowing anyone in on the grand scheme.

Jason began to reach out secretly to Lydia to see if Ronald had confided in her or see if she had been brought in to assist Ronald in some way. Lydia was as confused and frustrated as Jason about the lack of movement or lack of communication coming from Ronald. Lydia explained to Jason that she had other cases and even if she did not have other cases to work, she wasn't comfortable forcing her help onto Ronald. It was professional courtesy first and foremost, but also Ronald was a friend, and she did not want to encroach on that friendship. Furthermore, if Madison remained in the Maldives, nothing could be done. Jason reluctantly decided for the sake of his friendship to drop the matter and attempt to forget Madison Wilkes.

Ronald came for a visit one weekend and he and his girlfriend stayed at Jason's home. Jason's family and Ronald and his girlfriend had a relaxing weekend. The six of them visited the zoo, had dinner one evening, and Jason and Ronald grilled burgers and hot dogs one night. As the weekend ended and Ronald and his friend were putting their luggage in the car, Jason pulled Ronald to the side and spoke candidly with him.

"Listen man. I care about our friendship, and you mean a lot to Lindsey, myself, and the kids but I can't stop thinking about Madison Wilkes and the evil she perpetrated and has gotten away with. What the hell is going on? We went through a lot together on that damn case and have known each other way too long for you not to keep me in the loop. Talk to me man, talk to me. You said you might have a plan when we were told Madison had left the country. What was the plan? Is it still viable?"

"There is nothing to share. There are no new developments and right now, there is no path forward. I thought I had a plan, and it turned out to be a dead end. I made some phone calls and reached out to some people I thought could help and they could not. Don't think I have quit without making every possible effort. I'm not complacent about what happened and what Madison has done, but honestly, there is nothing I can do. I have the smallest canoe in the lake and the Feds can't even touch her. What the hell is a small-town sheriff in coastal Georgia going to do. I don't mean this callously nor hardhearted, but you need to make peace with the fact that this sick, psychotic bitch beat the system and got away. I'm not happy about it and this sounds horrible but in law enforcement, as in life, sometimes you have to accept defeat, learn from it, and move on. We had a great weekend and a lifelong friendship. Let's treasure that and try to forget. We will see you, Lindsey, and the girls soon. Please stay in touch and stop by Brunswick, if your delivery route takes you that way. I love ya brother."

As Ronald and his girlfriend stepped into the car and Ronald fired the engine and backed out of the driveway, Lindsey walked over to where Jason had not moved from where the two men had been discussing the Madison Wilkes' situation. Lindsey and Jason smiled as the two drove away and disappeared down the street and around the corner toward the interstate.

"What did you say to Ronald?"

"I thought he was as driven and upset about this as Lydia and I were. Now I don't know. He gave me some BS about accepting defeat and moving forward. That is not the guy I know nor the law enforcement officer I know. How could he just throw his hands up and say to hell with everything? The guy I knew would be turning over every stone imaginable until that bitch was behind bars."

"You have become obsessed with this Jason. I know you saw some horrible things and you may never forget the awful things she did, but maybe Ronald is right. You may have to move on, and hope karma catches up to Madison."

"I told something to Lydia one day and God help me if Ronald ever found out I thought and said this. She and I were talking about Madison and how there seemed to be no traction or action on the case by Ronald. I mentioned I was a little disappointed in the efforts and wished that efforts would be revisited. We spoke for a few minutes more and I guess she sensed that I had something else more pressing and difficult to say. Lydia pressed me on it and I just blurted it out. I told her that I hated feeling this way but there was a nagging thought that would not go away. I felt. Oh God help me. I felt as if Ronald might be on the take with Madison."

"Jason, you can't be serious. Ronald has been your friend for years and he helped you every step of the way to clear your name when you were wrongfully accused of this fiasco. You know better than that. Ronald is a faithful friend and law enforcement officer. You may have a thousand theories but this one you need to demolish and put to death."

Lindsey kissed Jason gently and wiped the tears off her face as she was visibly upset over what Jason had to say. She slowly walked to the front door and quietly slipped inside and closed the door. Jason moved slowly over the wooden swing hanging between the large oaks on the side of their home and sat down and began to swing. He sat there for hours looking off into space and mumbling to himself. He was ashamed of what he thought but the feeling would not go away. The yard light came on as the skies darkened and the moon began to shine. Jason slowly walked inside and went upstairs to go to bed. He would be back on the road making deliveries tomorrow and had resolutions he had to come to terms with.

A few weeks later, Jason was making a run to Birmingham and decided to stop in at a small diner just off the interstate on his way home for a quick bite to eat. He entered the diner and took a seat on a stool in front of the bar. After placing his order, Jason sent a quick text to Lindsey to let her know when he'd be home. He was enjoying the baseball game that was showing on the tiny television hanging over the bar area when suddenly a special news report interrupted the game. Jason turned white as a sheet as the special report laid out a story he could not believe or did not want to believe. The burly short-order cook gruffly said he did not want to listen to anymore of that news crud and was about to find another station with another game on. Jason remarked "STOP" almost at a yell as the cook grabbed the remote from behind the bar. The cook shot a glance at Jason and Jason lowered his tone and asked if he could please leave it at that station for a few more minutes. The cook grumbled something under his breath and returned the remote back to his position behind the bar.

The reporter spoke and Jason began to fumble in his shirt pocket for his cell phone. He was so shaken that he could barely press the numbers to call his wife. Lindsey answered in a panic as she, too, had seen a similar news report on the news station out of Atlanta. Jason stood up as the waitress brought out his meal. Jason thanked her and placed twenty dollars on the counter which would more than cover his meal and the tip. The waitress asked Jason if she could box up his lunch and he simply shook his head no. He made his way to the door and toward his rig.

"Can you believe this Lindsey? I thought about it, and I did not want to believe it. This person? Can it be true? I am going to call my dispatcher and make my way to Brunswick from here. I am not sure when I will be home, and I will call you when I have more information and can make sense of all of this."

Jason arrived in Brunswick seven hours later and parked his rig along the street across from the Glynn County Jail. He stepped inside the main office of the jail, gave his information and said who he needed to speak with. An officer took Jason through several locked doors and into a secure conference room within the jail area. The officer explained there was already someone with the prisoner. As the officer unlocked the door to the conference room, Jason saw Ronald sitting there. Jason paused for a second and took a deep breath. He was mortified. He slowly made his way over to the steel table and nervously sat down. His knees were almost knocking together as he stared in silent disbelief.

"Why did you do it? I saw the report on the television in Birmingham. I was mortified. I thought you were an honest, law-abiding, servant of the people. Now this. I cannot understand. Someone tell me this is a damn dream."

Ronald spun around from the end of the steel bench and faced Jason. "It is not a dream. What you saw in the news report is true. I wish it wasn't, and I could tell you it was one big misunderstanding, but it isn't. "

Jason was slowly beginning to regain his composure, and nervousness was being replaced with anger. "You worked alongside all those law officers and officials and were a part of this entire disgusting situation. How did Madison and Kelly get you involved in all of this? Was it money? Was it some type of power trip? How could you be so damn sick and twisted as those people?"

"You don't know anything about me, and you can judge me all you wish. I don't give a damn. The law never gave me anything but long hours and an opportunity for a worthless pension. Why don't you take your self-righteous ass out of her and take your buddy here with you?" Lydia Stringfellow slammed her hands down on the steel tabletop and angrily marched toward the door calling for the officer to return her to her cell.

As the officer unlocked the conference room door and escorted Lydia away, Jason finally spoke to Ronald after thirty or forty-five seconds of deafening silence. "Ronald, how in the hell could she do this man? She has worked with you on other cases and seemed like a dedicated officer of the law. She was passionate about catching Madison and Kelly and now it was all a charade. A damn performance by a gifted criminal. There is one good thing to come of this. She can now help con Madison to return to the United States or another country that has an extradition treaty so she can be arrested. That would earn Lydia a lighter sentence, right?"

"She refused to help us. I asked her before you arrived, and she told me she would rot in prison and in hell before she helped us do anything. She compared Madison to a folk hero among criminals and heralded her as a criminal mastermind. I am as shocked about all of this as you are. We prosecute her and hope maybe, someday, Madison makes a mistake.

CHAPTER 22

Closure

The trial for Lydia Stringfellow's sentencing was a two-week process, but the defense did not have much of a leg to stand on Lydia's defense.

She had been caught on tape with an overseas conspirator in which the two of them discussed the trafficking of several young girls, drugs, and cash. The jury deliberated less than eight hours and returned a unanimous verdict of guilty on all charges. Lydia had the opportunity to speak on her behalf during the sentencing phase and chose, again, not to implicate Madison or attempt to work with the authorities to assist in her potential capture.

The defense presented the judge with a myriad of legitimate cases where Lydia had shut down illegal operations and brought countless criminals to justice and felt her service could be considered in this matter. The judge heard arguments from the prosecution, also, and stated she would render her decision on sentencing in one week.

When Jason and Lindsey arrived at the Fulton County Courthouse, the trial and sentencing was held there as Lydia was a member of the GBI and the jurisdiction resided there, the parking lot was packed, and they had to park over half a mile away and walk to the building. Ronald had asked Jason to call him upon arrival and he would bring them inside the courthouse and the appropriate courtroom through a rear entrance. The three of them made their way inside the courthouse and toward courtroom five. They stood outside the door and awaited the opportunity to enter.

"Are you guys ready for this? I know this has been a long journey and you both may feel, like a lot of people, that the journey is not truly over," Ronald said almost apologetically.

"I am ready to see one more of this group go to prison, but not nearly as much as I would love to see Madison Wilkes behind bars. This helps and hurts. I'm ready to go inside and see what sentence the judge passes down to Lydia," Jason spoke with pain in his voice.

Jason, Lindsey, and Ronald stepped inside the courtroom and found spots along the adjacent wall with a relatively unobstructed view of the defense table and judge's seat. They could not see anyone seated at the prosecutor's desk or defense's but would see the defendant rise shortly when sentencing was handed down. The judge entered the courtroom and took his seat.

"I understand the defendant having been found guilty on all charges the parties have reached an agreement on the charges based on the cooperation of the defendant in the matter. The defendant has agreed to assist the authorities by naming contacts and providing information as to the specifics of the human trafficking routes and criminal enterprises where these people are kept until being sold or killed," Judge Phillips said.

Jason was thinking what Ronald and Lindsey had to be thinking. He thought Lydia had vehemently refused to name anyone in the organization nor assist on any level with the authorities. She must have had a change of heart over the last week, or someone must have done some heavy convincing when speaking with her. Jason was a little relieved at this news. This would help bring more people involved in this despicable enterprise to justice.

"The defendant will now rise, and I will render the sentencing to be imposed."

When the defendant rose, Jason and Lindsey nearly sank to the floor as their legs lost stability and their blood ran cold. This was not Lydia Stringfellow. Could it be who it appeared to be? Oddly, Ronald was unmoved at the sight of the unexpected defendant.

Judge Phillips continued once the defendant arose. "Madison Wilkes alias Roxanne Windermere, you are hereby sentenced to a term of no less than thirty years and no longer than your natural life without the possibility of parole. The facility to be determined by the Federal Bureau of Prisons. Bailiff, please escort the defendant to Federal Marshalls waiting in my chambers for transportation. This court is adjourned." Judge Phillips pounded his gavel and left the courtroom.

Jason, Linsdey, and Ronald watched as Madison Wilkes was escorted away and she showed no emotion while being removed from the courtroom. Her cold-blooded soul was vindictive to the core. Jason and Lindsey then looked at Ronald who had a wry, small smile running across his face.

Ronald grabbed Jason by the arm and motioned for Lindsey to follow them. "Lindsey, I need you to wait in the cafeteria area for Jason and me. I want to take him back to the main conference room and speak with him privately. He can fill you in later. I will have to swear him in as a temporary deputy again to allow his entrance into the conference room and participation in the discussions.

Lindsey nodded her head affirmatively and kissed Jason lightly on the check. She made her way towards the cafeteria and the two men made their way towards a small conference room at the end of the corridor. When they entered the conference room, a familiar face was seated at the table. It was Lydia Stringfellow, and she was in her street clothes and wearing her badge. Jason was now more perplexed than ever. He wanted to ask for an explanation, but his throat was so dry he couldn't speak. Ronald motioned for him to sit down, and he took a seat himself.

"Good afternoon, Jason. You look overly surprised to see me. I see my friend and fellow law enforcement officer Sheriff Watts here can still be trusted to maintain the integrity of an operation." Lydia smiled a small smile, extended her hand to Jason for a greeting, and winked at Ronald.

J"Ok. What the hell is going on here?" Jason asked with a crack in his voice. "A week ago, I saw you arrested and acting defiantly towards everyone and now you are seated here, wearing a badge, and Madison was just sentenced to thirty years in prison."

"Would you like to do the honors, Ronald?" Lydia now beaming brightly spoke.

"Relax, Jason and pay close attention. This was a little complicated and took some moving pieces to have everything you have witnessed today fall into place. I began to brainstorm, along with Lydia, almost immediately after Madison escaped to the Maldives. That pompous, arrogant, little tart had pissed us off something fierce. Every idea we could come up with was a dead end as we knew Madison is as crafty and intelligent as she is malicious. Lydia and I had almost given up hope when Lydia had one last idea. A couple of years ago she worked on a similar case where a female criminal had eluded the US authorities and had established a criminal enterprise and network in the Philippines. Lydia knew a person who worked as an undercover agent there and cooperated in the criminal's apprehension. His name is Ross Tosloc."

"Wait a second. Madison was in the Maldives, not the Philippines," Jason interrupted.

"As I say, it took a lot of moving pieces. We will get to where Ross fits into the puzzle shortly. We needed to appeal to Madison's greed and ego. She is crafty, intelligent, malicious, arrogant and greedy. She loves money and thinks she can get away with anything she puts her mind to. We had Lydia appear to join a criminal enterprise in the Philippines which specializes in human trafficking. She made several trafficking moves, all on paper of course. These trafficking moves showed buyers who spent enormous amounts of money on these ladies, well above what Madison and her cronies were being paid in North America.

"Here is where Ross Tosloc fits in the picture. He partners with another undercover agent in the Maldives named Jhoy Drinkwater. Jhoy is the perfect accomplice in our plan as she is native to the Maldives and has worked closely with the Philippines and other countries to destroy human trafficking. She knows how to navigate the surroundings and how the human trafficking networks operate.

"While Ross and Jhoy were formulating their part of the plan in Asia, Lydia and I were working on Lydia's arrest and our next step in the plan here. Lydia was found to be involved in human trafficking, arrested, tried, and convicted. A jury of her peers was never so accurate. We had twelve GBI agents on the jury. The defense attorneys work for the GBI. The prosectors work for the GBI. The judge was legit and knew of our plan and the reasoning behind it.

"We could not take a chance on a jury of ordinary citizens for two reasons. First, this was a mock proceeding and secondly, they might find Lydia not guilty, and we may not be able to get a second bite at the apple with another person arrested. Madison would get suspicious. Once we had everything loaded into the GBI's and FBI's database on Lydia's arrest, we conveniently allowed Ross Tosloc to breach the system and extract the names and major players in Lydia's human trafficking activity.

"These people are real per Mr. Tosloc and are being actively pursued and hopefully arrested once solid evidence can be leveraged against them. The real names of the players would allow Madison to do her homework and see that Lydia was into some heavy-duty criminal activities. In actuality, we set up a dummy database mirroring the GBI and FBI system but with this case and other fictitious cases we created and placed in the database."

"Why not just have Ross Tosloc breach the dummy system? Why all the trouble of a trial and staged convictions?"

"We needed Madison to see all the publicity on the television news and internet. We knew that a GBI agent being arrested for human trafficking would be on every news channel in the world and fly around the internet and social media. Now Lydia has been arrested, tried, and convicted and Ross Tosloc has breached our bogus system and retrieved Lydia's accomplices.

"The entire time we were working this angle, Jhoy Drinkwater had conveniently been networking with Madison for several weeks and enticing her with the large sums of cash that could be made in Asia versus North America and appealing to her appetite for the thrill of the game. Jhoy and Ross are truly experts and know how to play the game. Jhoy makes some dummy moves with law enforcement agents posing as captured human trafficking victims and she shows Madison the money transfers to her offshore accounts in the Caymans. Jhoy had her eating out of her hands.

"Madison was allowed to interact with the bogus traffickers in the Maldives and she kidnapped and sold some planted female agents to another set of bogus buyers who deposited cash into Madison's offshore accounts. These monies were budgeted and backed by the Maldives government and hoping they could retrieve the money once Madison was hopefully arrested. If not, they saw the lost money as money well spent in an effort to rid their nation of another trafficker.

"Now, we come to the most pivotal part of the plan. We need to introduce Madison to Ross Tosloc. Then Ross will need to persuade Madison to travel to the Philippines so she would be in a country in which she could be extradited. We were counting on her inflated ego and massive greed to allow her to think she could slip into the country unnoticed, conduct her trafficking plans, collect her money, and be back in the Maldives undetected.

"Ross and Jhoy played their parts beautifully. Ross provided Lydia's information he had breached from our bogus system through Jhoy to Madison, Madison had seen by now, we were sure, Lydia's arrest and conviction, and Jhoy would put Ross and Madison in communication with each other. Madison could not resist the temptation of the large sums of money she saw Lydia making based on those bogus reports.

"When she spoke with Ross, he convinced her he had so many criminal activities that he could not possibly manage anything further and especially the level of movement Lydia had been involved with. Madison was swallowing all this hook, line, and sinker.

"The time had come for Madison to travel to the Philippines and transact her first trafficking event. She arrived on a freightliner out of the Maldives which was delivering imports to the Port of Manilla. Passengers were allowed on this freightliner, and no identification was required, just a cash transaction for the ticket. Once she arrived in Manilla, Ross arranged for helicopter transportation from Manilla to the island of Leyte where he and his team, along with several FBI agents, would be waiting for her.

"The helicopter landed and Madison was greeted by our agents and Ross' team. Ross was arrested so he could continue his undercover operation, and he agreed to help capture Jhoy Drinkwater to further perpetuate the ruse in front of Madison.

"The agents stated she cried like a baby and begged for lenience and forgiveness. She was transported to the United States, handcuffed to an FBI agent on the flight to ensure there would be no means of escape.

"The sentencing you saw today was a plea agreement she reached for her assistance and avoidance of the death penalty as she was linked to murders and charged with the murder of Kelly Parton. Madison put up a solid front for a day or so but she sang like canary once she was informed about the death penalty. This sick, twisted soul will probably never see the outside of a prison again but if she does it will be with an ankle monitor attached and strict probationary terms. She has thirty years before she can cross that bridge. "

"I'll be damned. This was the craziest thing I have ever heard. You guys had me thinking you were both involved at one time. I am sorry for questioning your character. You guys played the roles so well, you even had me fooled. I am glad she is behind bars and

FBI have leads on all of her sick cohorts. Great work you guys," Jason said with a sigh of relief.

Lydia stood up and looked at both men. "Want to go say goodbye to an old friend?"

The three friends walked out the door and decided to ride down to the Federal Building and see Madison Wilkes one last time. They deserved the opportunity to see her in bondage just like the poor souls she had placed in bondage over the years.